FROST

Kathryn James

h
Hodder
Children's
Books

A division of Hachette Children's Books

For Leo Rocky Allison – the littlest of us all.

INVERCLYDE LIBRARIES

Also by Kathryn James,
read the spellbinding:

Mist

One

Something woke Nell.

Heart hammering, she sat up and wrapped her old fur coat around her. She'd laid it on her bed last night for extra warmth. It still smelled of pine needles.

Something was wrong, but she didn't know what. In the darkness her radio alarm showed 6 a.m., which meant there was a long time to go before dawn.

Maybe the snowstorm had woken her – or the cold. She'd gone to bed in all her clothes, because the weather forecast had warned of temperatures down to minus ten. The New Year was two days old and it had brought a big freeze.

There it was again! Someone was throwing stones at her window.

She pulled the blind up and tried to look out, but there was frost on the inside of the glass even though the central heating had been on all night. She scraped a hole, freezing her fingertip.

A figure was standing in the garden, looking up. For a heart-stopping moment she thought it was Evan.

Evan, the mystery boy who became her friend, who wasn't human, who came from another world and rocked hers.

But it wasn't him. It was too small, and anyway he was somewhere in a wilderness far to the North. He'd been there two months and three days, and she'd begun to realize she might never see him again.

The figure waved to her, urgently, and then ran.

She pulled on her new boots and rushed out of her bedroom, stepping quickly over a boy lying on the landing, wrapped in a blanket. Her sister's door was open. She could see five bodies squashed on to Gwen's bed. Another two were on a lilo on the floor, wearing their coats.

Downstairs, she tiptoed through the living room. Each sofa had a tightly huddled couple, wrapped in quilts. The only sound, besides breathing, was faint gunfire coming from the computer by the front window. Two blanket-draped boys were slumped by it, playing some kind of game online, as though they'd been there all night.

It was party time at Gwen's.

All her friends were crashing here, because Jackie,

their mum, was working overtime. The emergency services were at full stretch because of the freak weather.

She picked her way quickly through the bodies lying on a futon on the floor, treading on a couple of them. They twitched and turned over, pulling the covers round themselves and scattering cans and bottles. There was a Post-it note stuck on the TV that hadn't been there last night. It was a threat from Mum. She must have called in during the night, whilst she was on patrol.

Gwen! Get these people out before I get back. Or else!!
I said four friends round – max!!!

Her sister was curled like a kitten in one of the armchairs. Her head came up sleepily as Nell crept by.

'Wassup? What time is it?'

'Early. Six. Go back to sleep.'

'Where you going?'

'For a walk.'

'Weirdo. You'll freeze to death.'

Gwen slumped back down and closed her eyes, but a blonde head popped up from the other armchair. Nell could just make out that it was Becca, Gwen's best friend.

'Six o'clock! Frick. I should've gone home last night! I'm working for Dad today. He'll kill me!' She began to scrabble round for her boots, treading on the sleeping bodies and making them moan horribly.

Nell fled. The front door was sealed with snow and ice and needed a kick to open it. She stepped over the Christmas tree, now lying half buried next to the wheelie bin. Her front garden and the whole of Woodbridge Road had been obliterated by the snow.

The stone thrower was waiting for her under the streetlamp. She could see that it was a young girl in a fur jacket and hood, leggings and boots. A few thin white plaits peeked out from under the hood.

'Star!' said Nell, shocked. *Evan's cousin, the little witch-healer, standing in her street!*

'Can you hear?' the Elven girl cried.

'Hear what?'

But Star was off again and running down the street. Something terrible must have happened, to bring her into this world. Nell crunched and slithered after her, down the road to the church then into the alley that led to the woods. Star was waiting at the entrance, hopping up and down impatiently, but something had caught Nell's eye. The alley was choked with snow. It had fallen last night and covered any footprints of the day before – so why was she staring at three fresh sets of prints?

The small ones were Star's. Then a bigger set. The third

looked as though it might be boots with a heel. Who wore heels in the woods, in weather like this?

'Who else is with you?' she called.

'No one. Just me.' Star was jumping up and down, urging her on. 'Please! Can't you hear it?'

Nell listened, but she couldn't hear anything.

She wrapped her coat tight round herself, wishing she'd remembered her gloves, and ran into the woods after Star. It looked like a deadly winter wonderland, the snow lying deep between the trees, the branches etched with snow and frost.

She hadn't been back here since Evan left. She'd concentrated on her schoolwork instead and amused herself by letting her so-called friends, Paige and Bria, know that she couldn't care less about them any more.

Now she followed Star, slipping and slithering towards the hollow where the mist lay. The path down to it was a sheet of ice. She hung on to a branch as she skidded down, and got a shower of snow down her neck. Then the mist was sparkling before her like the tinsel on their Christmas tree. The stepping stones shone with ice.

Star was already dancing ahead of her, disappearing into the mist.

Nell put her foot on the first slippery stone. She could still remember the sequence of steps that would take her through to the place that had haunted her dreams for the last two months. She'd never forget. Nor would she forget the way the mist began to thicken around her as though trying to push her back, or the feeling of vertigo as though she was walking over a chasm.

She fought her way through and emerged into the clearing. The cold was even more intense here. It hit her as though someone had left a deep-freezer door open and the tears in her eyes were turning to ice.

The clearing was deep in snow, and all around were pine trees, the ones that had scented her coat so deeply. This was the other forest, the one that was outside the world, the one that belonged to the hidden people, the Elven. This was the dangerous secret that she kept. Icicles a foot long hung from the branches and wolf tracks criss-crossed from side to side. Between the trees other patches of mist winked and twinkled at her, each one a gateway to another place.

Star was standing forlorn in the middle, her breath crystallizing in a cloud before her. Her hood was thrown back and her white plaits were shining under the Elven moon.

'I helped you,' she cried. 'Now you have to help us. There's no one else.'

Nell went over to her, sinking to her knees in the soft

powder snow, and grabbed Star's hands. They were like ice. 'What is it?'

'It's happened too quickly. Can't you hear it?' whispered Star. 'Listen.'

She listened but she couldn't hear anything. 'I don't know what you mean.'

Then her heart gave a thump. Oh Lord. That was it. *She couldn't hear anything*. There was nothing. Not even the creak and rustle of the trees now they were laden with snow. Just a silence. A deep, frozen silence.

'The harps,' she said, horrified. 'The harps have stopped singing.'

No more music, no more never-ending melodies from the huge devices spread through the forest, which kept the Elven land from breaking up and dying.

'The ice is spreading from the lake. And we've seen Ice Elven.' Star's face went even paler than its normal milk-white. 'They're the bad ones, Nell! They're so frozen their hearts don't beat.'

'What can I do?' said Nell.

Star's hands squeezed hers desperately. 'You have to go and find Evan.'

Becca made it to the shop on time. Cutler's Antique Jewellery in the town centre was the family business.

She'd left her dad parking the car, but she needn't have hurried; no one was out shopping, not in this weather.

Except for the boy sitting in the doorway, hugging his knees.

She almost didn't notice him. He was dressed in shades of pale grey, like shadows on the white snow. He blended. He had a grey hoodie with the sleeves pushed up and the zip half down as though he was hot, instead of freezing to death. There was another shade of grey for his jeans, another for his boots.

When he saw her he leaped to his feet, happy as a puppy.

'I've been waiting for you to open,' he said, brightly. He sounded slightly foreign.

Becca pulled off her fluffy beret and tucked a strand of her bed-hair behind her ear. He was definitely sweet. He was her age, maybe, or younger, and his face wasn't that special, but somehow it was startling. He had skin like a pearl, as though he'd never seen the sun. She couldn't stop staring, and when he pushed his hood back and she saw his shiny black hair, like a raven's feathers, she could hardly stop herself wanting to stroke it. She liked the style it was in. It didn't look as though he'd been to the hairdresser's, or had spent hours in front of the mirror with gel. It looked like it grew that way.

His eyes were the lightest grey, too, like pale silver. He was shading them with his hand as though the day was too bright. It wasn't – in the last half-hour the sky had turned purple like a bruise. There was another snowstorm on the way.

'Lots of other shops are open,' she said. 'You didn't need to sit here, freezing.'

'This one. I want this shop.' He grinned at her, eager and friendly, and wrinkled his nose. 'Let me in.'

She shouldn't, she should wait for her dad, she had to think of security. But this cute puppy-boy was hardly a threat, so she opened the door and switched off the alarm. The shop was dark, the security blinds still down. He followed her in and looked around. Their breath smoked, it seemed colder in here than outside. She switched on the electric heater.

'Aren't you cold?' she said.

Close to, his skin looked as though it was covered in a thin layer of frost that glittered.

He shrugged. 'No. I love it. Where I come from it's much colder.'

'Must be the Arctic, then.'

'Aha,' he said, in a singsong way. 'Not really. But far away.' He looked around. 'I've been wanting to come here. It'll be fun.'

He started leaping round the place looking at the displays, cooing at the jewellery as if he was in love with gold. If Gwen and the rest of the girls were here, they'd be petting him, he was so adorable.

She went to lift the blinds.

'Don't. It's too bright. I like the darkness.'

For a moment she couldn't tell where his voice came from. She'd lost sight of him. The shop wasn't big, but she had to concentrate before she could pick him out in the gloom. He was definitely good at blending into shadows. He was standing in front of one of the display cabinets, like a child at the pick and mix, his nose almost touching the glass.

'I want that ring,' he breathed.

The object of his passion sat on a velvet cushion under a spotlight in the centre of the display, a snaky spiral of gold, with two tiny but perfect rubies for eyes.

'Right. Course you do!' She smiled at him, she couldn't help herself. As though he'd got money to buy stuff like that! 'That's the Elf ring. My dad says the goldwork is so incredibly fine and the jewels so expertly cut, it must be the work of elves.'

'Elven,' he said, absently, without taking his eyes off the ring.

'Sorry?'

'Elven, not elvish, elf or elves. It's always Elven.'

'He's only joking, it's not true,' she said, puzzled by his sudden seriousness.

He gave a start. 'Aha – of course,' he agreed, happily.

Side by side, they admired it.

'It's a serpent ring, made to coil around your finger.'

'I love it, I adore it,' he said. 'Where did you get it from?'

She didn't answer straight away because he'd picked up the black feather that her dad used to clean dust off the rings and was brushing it absent-mindedly against his white cheek. For a moment or two she was mesmerized. She wanted to keep him there, until Gwen turned up, so they could watch him together!

'This man came in a couple of years ago, and sold it to us,' she said. He was listening intently, nibbling the feather with perfect white teeth now. 'It isn't for sale. Dad keeps it on display because he loves it.'

'Did the man give his name?' he asked.

'Yes. There's a label on the box. Look. Thorn. That's all we know.'

'Can I try it on?'

She found herself looking straight into his silver eyes. They now had a slightly tricky feline quality.

'No. Not allowed. You'll have to wait for my dad.'

He wrinkled his nose at her and looked slightly cross. Even that was sweet.

'He won't be long. Are you new round here?'

'Aha.' That seemed to be his way of saying yes.

She suddenly had a good idea. 'Well, keep it quiet, but we're having a snow party tonight. The caretaker forgot to lock the school pavilion and we're crashing there. Come along.'

He carried on looking round. 'Who's going?'

'Everyone. My bezzie mate Gwen, and the girls and . . .'

He whirled round, suddenly intense. '. . . and Nell?'

'Yeah, suppose.' For a moment she wondered how he knew Gwen's little sister, then the thought was gone. 'Anyway never mind her, you wait till you meet our gang.'

He gave a laugh. It was like ice breaking. 'Shame, but I can't. It's forbidden. I'm here for the gold, only.'

She frowned, disappointed. 'Hope you've got a lot of money, then.'

He laughed again. 'No, I'm not going to buy anything! I'm Loki Thorn. I came to get our ring back.' He looked around, his eyes alight. 'And I might as well take all the other sparkly things, too.'

Becca put her hands on her hips. Was this some kind of joke? 'OK, so you're sweet, but really, who do you think you are?'

He carried on looking in the display cases. 'Sleep,' he said, casually, with a wave of one hand.

Becca dropped like a stone. He bent down and whispered in her ear.

'Sorry, pretty girl, but I'm your nightmare. I can make you dream whatever I want.' He leaned closer and whispered some more.

Then he began breaking the glass on all the cases, ignoring the alarm that started to sing out shrilly. He took everything and was out of the shop before Becca's father had time to race round the corner.

As Mr Cutler later told the police, all he heard were the sounds of two people laughing and swiftly running footsteps, as the snow began to fall like a white curtain once more.

Two

Nell stood in the Elven forest, feeling far from her own world. Her teeth were beginning to chatter.

'Which one is it?' she said.

In front of her were ten patches of mist between the trees. Each like a magic door, leading to another place. Alaska, Canada, Sweden, Siberia, cold northern countries where the great-families of Elven used to live, before the Watchers started putting them in the iron camps.

Star pointed. 'That one.'

So that was the mist that led to Siberia, the wildest of all the places. And to Kamchatka, the most far away part of that freezing land. This was where Evan was trying to rescue his family and the other Elven.

Nell had seen the camp on Google Earth. It was a collection of buildings like a refugee camp crossed with a college campus. They had all the facilities, a school, apartments and dining halls, Evan had said, because the Watchers weren't that cruel. All the Elven didn't have was freedom. The black lines surrounding the camp that she'd seen on Google Earth were iron fences, metres high. There was no need for anything more, because iron was poison to the Elven. It sapped their strength, it muddled their thoughts. It made them safe and unthreatening. And that's how the humans who knew about the Elven liked them. Otherwise they might try and take the world back by using their powers of charm.

Seeing that the Elven were supposed to be so threatening, Nell thought they'd been overcome and captured very easily.

'Take me through,' she said.

Star took her hand and they walked into the mist.

Beneath her feet were stepping stones that had to be danced over, but these were not white stones that glowed like the moon, like the ones in her mist. These were black, shiny stones. As she followed Star's lead, she slipped and nearly fell when the vertigo hit her. She was in no-man's-land, between the Elven world and her world. She clutched Star's hand.

'What happens if I fall?' she muttered, as she copied Star and hopped and skipped from stone to stone, as the mist thickened and clung to her face like tentacles.

'Mama used to say you go somewhere else and never come back,' said Star. She did one last hop and stopped. 'Anyway, we're here.'

They walked out of the mist on to the edge of a thin forest of spindly bare trees and hard-packed snow. Nell blinked and gasped. The forest was nothing compared to the view beyond it. She stayed in the shelter of the last trees and looked out over a vast landscape. It was as though she could see to the end of the world.

Spread before her was a land of mountains and dead volcanoes, sprinkled with thin forests and glaciers. The sky looked like glass. The wind that was blowing into her face was so cold it was making her teeth ache.

Evan was out there? The thought made her feel sick.

'They have Faolan and another wolf with them,' said Star in a small voice. A tear fell on her cheek, froze instantly and blew away in little icy particles.

Two months, he'd been gone, with his cousin Falcon. Nell had been thinking about it since he left. The camp was fenced with iron. They couldn't just open the gates. They couldn't climb over the top. How were they going to storm it? Did they even have a plan?

She bear-hugged her arms round herself, as the wind continued to find any little gap to blow through and freeze her. 'Have you heard from him?'

Star felt in her pocket. 'He sends the wolves back with messages.'

She pulled a print out of her pocket. It was an image of the camp, in colour but still everything looked black and white and grey. She saw tall iron fences and beyond them, blurred faces, white hair, white faces. Out of focus in the foreground was the muzzle of Faolan, Evan's wolf.

'They've tried everything – trying to get the native people to help, digging tunnels, trying to ambush the guards. Nothing's worked yet.'

Tunnelling? Just Evan and Falcon? It would take them forever. That's why they weren't back.

Star began to cry as she carefully folded the picture and put it back in her pocket. 'See, I can't wait for him to send Faolan back again!' she cried. She clutched Nell's hands. 'We have to let him know about the harps now. This minute!'

Nell bent down. There were footsteps frozen in the packed snow.

'Evan's from two months ago?'

Star shrugged. 'Maybe.'

Nell followed them but they faded out after a few metres. It would make no difference if they'd carried on. She couldn't follow him. She met Star's anxious eyes.

'He could be anywhere. I don't know how to find him.'

She looked at the vast landscape. The trees on the slope opposite looked like tiny twigs. The mountains were even farther away. 'I can't flit. It would take me forever to search.'

Star blinked, her mouth a straight line. Nell could see she was trying not to cry. Elven girls and boys were tough, even the little ones. Look at the way she was caring for all her little cousins, and she was only about eleven. There must be another way, she thought. There's always another way.

'Let me think.'

She needed a way to find a boy in the middle of a wilderness the size of Europe, who was hiding beside a camp that was a mere speck amidst snow, ice and endless mountains. Think, Nell, think. That's what you're supposed to be good at.

He would be holed up near the camp. She needed to get a message to the camp and then to him. How? The camp would have a phone. If only she could somehow get a call through to him.

She stared at the hostile land for a few more moments, the bitter wind battering her face and making her eyes stream with tears. When she finally turned to Star, her mouth was almost too frozen to talk.

'There's another way. But you won't like it.'

The Elven girl was trying to huddle out of the wind behind a tree. 'Anything.'

'I can ask my nan to help.'

Star's eyes widened. 'The Watcher woman? No! She'll tell them to find Evan and they'll capture him and Falcon. They'll lock them away in the iron camp as well. And what will become of the rest of us?'

Nell forced her frozen face to smile a little. 'Trust me. I made everything work out last time, didn't I?'

Star looked everywhere but at her, then kicked the snow around at her feet for a while.

'Suppose,' she said at last.

'Good,' said Nell. 'Now, can we get out of this wind, before I die of cold.'

Star led her back through the mist to the Elven forest, which was even colder than Siberia, but it didn't have wind that blew straight through your flesh and bones. A silence still reigned, but it wasn't empty any more.

Standing in the clearing, their breath creating an icy cloud around them, were a bunch of Elven children. The youngest were sitting bundled up in furs on sledges, whose strings were held by the older ones.

This was Evan's great-family – all that was left of them. They were his youngest cousins. There was little Bean, Falcon's brother, who'd made friends with her last time.

And Pixie and Fay, two cute little girls, who were huddled on one sledge. This was being pulled by Lily, who'd tossed her long hair back and glared at Nell when they'd first met, but who was now looking at her hopefully from the small space left between her hat and scarf. Behind them were – Nell frowned and then remembered their names, Sky and Crystal and Storm. And scowling at her, the two soldier boys, Rex and Bran, still in combat gear, but Arctic pattern now.

'Hi,' she said, feeling overwhelmed at so many eyes staring at her. It was like having to speak in assembly at school but much worse. These were expecting more from her than a reading or a thank you for a class prize.

'So, can you go get him?' said Rex, not sounding very hopeful.

'I've got a better idea.'

She didn't have time to say anything else. The ground beneath their feet began to tremble, shaking the snow into a haze that covered the ones on the sledges. Nell put her hand out to save herself. It felt as though the land was about to be shaken and torn to pieces around her.

'What's happening?' she shouted, as the older Elven crouched down and hung on to the little ones, or tried to cover their ears.

Suddenly something screeched like a violin playing the wrong note, but a million times louder. Birds flew up out of the pine trees, sending snow cascading. The Elven howled in fear. The littlest ones screamed in competition. Nell clutched her ears in agony, as the note stretched on and on, setting her teeth on edge like a steel stool dragged across stone tiles.

Star put her hands round her mouth and shouted, 'It's the harp. It's dying.'

Her hands trembling like the ground, Nell fumbled in her pocket for her phone and flicked it to record. She held it out; the noise went on and on for over a minute, then came down a few octaves and became like something played badly on penny-whistles, if penny-whistles were as loud as jet engines. This was what the haunting melody of the harps had become. Finally it stopped, and all that was left was the sound of the littlest Elven snivelling and the disturbed birds cawing to each other in fright.

'It keeps doing that,' said Star, looking terrified. 'It's all that's left of the music. And each time the earthquake gets worse and the screech gets shorter. We don't have much time.'

The others came crowding round them, now the ground had stopped shaking.

'We're scared we're going to die,' said Pixie, clutching her sleeve. When she'd first met them, all Pixie and Fay had wanted was bubble-gum, now they wanted her to save their lives.

'Or we might freeze and become ice, like the Ice Elven,' said Fay.

'Our hearts will stop like theirs,' said Pixie.

Star gathered them close to her. 'Nell's going to help us. You'll see.'

Which made everyone stare at her again. Nell took a deep breath and stared back, meeting every single pair of charcoal eyes this time.

'I have a plan.' She managed a smile. 'Leave it to me. I'm on to it.'

Tick, *tick*, *tick*, went the clock.

Nell held out her frozen hands to the fire. One of the blazing logs settled and blew out a blast of heat.

All she had to do was ask her nan for a favour.

Her grandmother's house stood on its own on the other side of the woods from Nell's. If she went over the back fence of her garden, and straight through the trees, it was only a mile away, but she and Gwen weren't supposed to go into the woods after the 'incident'. So she had to walk along the road that ran around the outside. It had taken her so long she'd almost lost faith in her idea by the time the Red House came into sight. It was called the Red House because it was streaked in rust and when it rained it wept red tears. That was because its bones were made of iron, and most of the outside was covered in iron, too.

This had been the home of the Watchers for hundreds of years, protected from the Elven by the stink and sting of iron. Now it was home to Druscilla Church, Nell's nan, and the present Watcher for these woods and this particular patch of mist. Nell had grown up on the porch out the back, playing near the woods, never knowing that her grandmother was responsible for policing the Elven. To become a Watcher you had to be immune to the Elven charm, a power they had that could alter human thoughts and make humans forget. This immunity ran in the family. Her dad had it, so did she. It was probably why she'd always been close to her grandmother and able to talk to her, when usually she was tongue-tied.

Not this time, though. There'd been lots of silences since she'd knocked on the door, and not much talking.

Dru was sitting in the chair by the fire. She looked the same, with her usual long grey plait down her back, and her biker boots and her no-nonsense face – but something had changed. She looked as though someone

24

had kicked half the life out of her. Nell had never seen her look so dejected.

'How was Christmas?' Dru asked.

'Weird.'

Mum and Dad were talking, which was unusual, but Dad wasn't talking to Nan. It was the first time Nell had seen her since Gwen was found in the woods. There'd been no Boxing Day dinner at the Red House this year. No cosy visits for mince pies and stockings round the big old fireplace. Dru had dropped their presents off, and they'd sent some back, but that was it.

'For me, too.' Dru gave her a searching look. 'How's it been since you discovered the big secret?'

She meant since Nell had found out about the Elven.

'Like I'm only half here. Half of me is wondering what's going on in their world.' She didn't mention Evan's name. Not to Nan. Not yet. Evan and his brother's plan to kidnap her sister had started the near-tragedy.

Dru nodded. 'That's how it is. Once you know, you're torn between two worlds. You're not properly human any more, but you're nowhere near being Elven.' She thumped the arm of her chair. 'Damn. I wish none of this had happened.'

Nell fiddled with a ring on her finger, twisting it this way and that. 'I don't mind.'

'You will.'

A silence fell again. The clock ticked loudly to fill it, joined now by the sound of a keyboard being bashed in the next room. Someone else was here in the Red House. Someone Nan hadn't introduced, which was unusual. Something else had changed, too.

'Where's the photos of the Elven gone, Nan?'

Last time she'd stood in this room there'd been a line of photos, like at the police station – Britain's most wanted. Evan, his brother Fen, Star and Falcon.

Dru stared bleakly into the fire. 'Things have changed, since you came back through the mist,' she said, bitterly. 'My boss, Stan Larson, the one you met, has taken away most of my duties.'

'Because you stuck up for me?'

'Yes.'

'Sorry.'

'Don't be.' Dru tried to smile. 'I gave my life to the Watchers, and it turned me into something I wasn't. A hard-hearted policewoman. I helped make rules for others that I didn't want to keep when it came to my granddaughters.'

'Are they going to sack you?' said Nell.

'Maybe. Now I have a tracker on my bike. I have to report where I go.' Dru nodded at the wall where the

26

keyboard bashing was filtering through. 'I don't have the PC any more. I have to relay any communications through the new Watcher.'

Nell pointed to a bag tucked away behind Dru's chair. 'You've got a laptop. And Wi-Fi.'

Dru smiled for the first time. 'You're sly, Nell. You notice everything.'

'Like you. And Dad. Don't worry, he'll start talking to you again, in the end. He's angry that he nearly lost Gwen, that's all.'

Dru said nothing. She just sat and stared into the fire. Nell knew it was now or never. She had to ask for her favour.

'You went to the Kamchatka camp,' she said, trying to sound casual. 'Do you still know people there?'

'Yes, why?'

'Do they know you're in trouble with your boss?'

'No. Not yet. It's not general knowledge.' She sighed and looked at Nell. 'What's all this about?'

Secretly, Nell crossed her fingers. She took a deep breath. 'Um. I need to get a message to Evan. He's outside the Kamchatka camp.'

Dru's face changed. It became stern and guarded at the mention of Evan's name. 'And how come he's outside a secret camp?' she demanded.

'It's not important.' Nell forced herself to keep her chin up and stare back. 'He just is, OK? But I need to tell him something. It's life and death, honest.'

Dru shook her head. 'No way. Not again. Last time you nearly died because you stayed in their world too long. It's poison to us. *They're* poison to us. You keep out of Elven affairs, do you hear me?'

She stood up and was ready to stomp off to the kitchen, but Nell jumped up and stood in her path. 'No. I won't. I have to do this. And you owe me. You owe Gwen.' Nell hardened her heart. 'You nearly let her get stolen away for ever.'

Dru winced at the mention of the kidnapping.

'Yes. I'll pay for that until my dying day.' Her eyes became suspiciously bright. 'That's why I can never do anything again to put you girls in danger.'

'This won't,' said Nell, quickly. 'You'll be doing it for someone else. To save lives. When doctors save people they don't ask whether they're good or bad, they just save them. Same here. Ask no questions, but *please* just do this one thing for me.'

A silence fell. The clock ticked on. It matched her thumping heart.

'Just a message, Nan. Words only. Promise. No danger to me.'

Dru hesitated, then shook her head. 'No danger to you. But I'd be breaking even more rules that I swore to uphold—' she began.

The door opened and a head popped round it. The new Watcher, Nell presumed. Dru stared blankly for a moment, then said, 'What?'

'I've just had a call. The boss is coming down in a couple of hours,' said the woman. 'He's got a few VIPs from the government with him. It's private, so, um, it's probably best if you were out.'

Dru stiffened. 'This is my house. I can come and go as I please.'

The woman raised her eyebrows. 'It's the Watcher's house, actually. And I'm the acting Watcher at the moment. Sorry, Druscilla. So if you wouldn't mind giving us a bit of space?' The door closed.

Dru's face was like steel now. Without saying another word she got the laptop out from behind the chair, set it on the coffee table and powered it up. 'Let's do it,' she said, grimly. 'What's the message?'

Nell took her phone out of her pocket and pressed a few buttons. Anything but meet her nan's eyes, which were very sharp and seemed to be able to look right through into people's minds and see if they were lying. 'It's just a little recorded message from his cousins. They

29

want to know if he's all right because of the bad weather.' She paused. 'So do I, actually.'

She held her breath. Would Nan buy it? She could feel her stare. Then Dru made a noise like *pffff*.

'You! My sensible granddaughter,' she said. 'You've gone and fallen for an Elven, haven't you?'

Nell felt herself go red. 'Not necessarily.'

Dru shook her head. 'Those blimmin' Rivers boys,' she muttered. 'Take it from me, Nell, don't bother with that Evan. Find a human boy, if you have to go sweet on someone.'

If she hadn't been so desperate Nell would've been praying the floor would open up and swallow her. She would've run off and not come back.

Ha, but it's so true, said a little voice in her mind.

Well, she would use it, then. She would let her nan think she was pining for Evan. She put on her soppiest face and put her hands together as though praying.

'Please. Please. Please, Nan. Just this once. Then I'll try to forget about him.'

Dru gave her a searching and suspicious look, and said, 'Hmmmph. And how am I going to get a message to an Elven boy who is outside the camp?'

'You'll think of something,' said Nell. 'You're clever.'

They both knelt in front of the laptop. Skype

bleeped up on to the screen.

'I'm sure I'm being fooled,' she said, grimly. 'But there you go, it's ringing the Kamchatka camp. The wonders of modern technology. When I was born we were lucky to have a phone in the house. Now all they're used for is to locate everyone's mobile.'

Skype blooped. Dru's call had been answered. The screen turned from blue to a clear picture of a bearded man. He said something, but Nell could hardly understand him, his Russian accent was so thick. Dru had no problems.

'Fedor!' She smiled into the laptop camera.

The man smiled back through his beard. 'Dru? Hey, waddaya know! Some surprise.'

Dru kept the smile going. 'How's things at the camp?'

He leaned to one side, the webcam jiggled. It showed a window and through it, the outside world of snow and dark oblong shapes that were the buildings for the Elven and the guards. 'Same as usual, here. Nothing changes.'

'Hear anything from the boss?' said Dru, innocently.

Nell crossed her fingers and held her breath. If Fedor knew Dru had been sacked, then her plan would fail.

'Larson? He doesn't bother to ring us!' said Fedor, cheerfully. 'Out of sight, out of mind, like the Elven here.'

'Any disturbances?'

31

'Maybe. Footprints outside. Could be hunters. And we've got a couple of wolves hanging round.' Nell caught her breath. Please let it be Faolin. 'So what's up, Dru?'

Dru kept her voice wonderfully innocent. Nell was impressed. 'I'm retiring at last, Fedor. Letting someone else take over. I'm ringing to say goodbye to everyone – you and Paul and Stefan, and Rita in the guardhouse and Lana and Maria. Have you still got the Tannoy system up? This connection's not good, so it would be better to send a message to all of you at the same time.'

'Sure. I'll hook you up.' The line took on an echo. 'I'll patch you into the CCTV system, too, so you can see everyone.' The picture on the screen changed to one of the camp, looking down from above. Nell could see the buildings, the loudspeakers on tall poles, children running about on the hard-packed snow, and some Elven strolling about. In the distance she could see the high fences, black criss-crossing lines against the white. A guard was standing near one, flapping his arms and bear-hugging himself to keep warm. 'I'll be sad to see you go, Dru. You were the only one who cared that we were doing our best here.'

'I know, Fedor. I'll miss you, too. You made things less prison-like. You've been good.'

'OK. When you're ready.'

Dru nudged her.

This was it. It was now or never. She clicked play on her phone and held it near the mike. The screech of the dying harps echoed down the connection, up to a satellite orbiting the earth, down again to Kamchatka and out through the speakers. The terrible sound poured over the camp, echoing out over the fence and across the snowfields.

Dru swore and sat back on her heels.

'Whoa!' shouted Fedor.

His face came back into view but not before Nell saw the figures of the Elven stop and look up. 'We got a bad connection, Dru!' He laughed. 'That set the wolves howling! Listen.'

In the background Nell could hear a distant frenzied howling. She crossed her fingers. Please let that mean Evan is near. Let him hear the screech of the harps. Please let him understand.

Dru pushed Nell out of the way quickly, pretending to press a few keys, her face an artful mix of surprise and annoyance. 'Yes. Some kind of feedback, I think.' She was having trouble keeping her voice from shaking. 'Sorry about that, Fed. I'll call you back later, when I've sorted it.'

She shut down Skype with a click, closed the laptop

and leaped to her feet. But Nell was even faster. She pulled her gloves on and backed towards the door.

'Oops. The recording must've got screwed up. Never mind. Got to go.'

'Oh my God. I know what that was!' Dru was horrified. 'A musical instrument gone out of key. But not a normal instrument, something huge. Come back here, this minute!'

No way, thought Nell. She had another plan to put into action now. One that involved going to Gwen's snow party.

'Bye, Nan,' she said, and ran for it.

Three

Nell knocked on the door. The winter dark had fallen in the middle of the afternoon, now it was night. Which meant it was teeth-chatteringly cold.

A muffled, suspicious voice said, 'Password?'

Nell shivered, even though she was wrapped in three jumpers, a woolly hat pulled down to her eyebrows and a red scarf knitted by her mum to prove she wasn't always at work. It had stitches missing, but it was so cool.

'It's me,' she said.

'Who?'

'Me! Let me in, Becca, before I freeze.'

She breathed on her hands as she waited for the door to open. The old sports pavilion was on the far side of the school's playing fields, next to the river. It was an ancient wooden building, creaking and rotten, but now it was iced like a wedding cake with frost and snow. No one used it since they built the new hi-tech sports hall close to the school. And no one lived near to hear the music, or see the groups of partygoers who'd been arriving for the last half-hour.

The door opened. Warmth billowed out. 'Oh, it's you.'

Becca looked different. Her hair was normally long and shiny, but she'd got it tied up in a ponytail as though she hadn't bothered with the straighteners. And her eyes weren't her normal panda eyes. In fact she looked like she'd just got out of bed and done nothing to her face. Nell slipped past her into a room already crowded and hot, and reeking of the lethal-looking punch a group of boys were brewing on a camping stove.

Becca closed the door and leaned on it.

'Did you see anyone? A boy?'

Nell took off her hat and unwrapped her scarf. What was Becca going on about? Of course boys were heading this way. They always did for Becca and Gwen's parties. 'I saw plenty.'

'No, this special boy. Got hair that, you know, goes just right.' Becca frowned, as though trying to remember something. 'And he's hard to see in the snow.'

'What're you going on about?'

'Never mind.' Becca waved her away irritably, and yawned as she took up her position as doorkeeper

36

again. 'I'm tired, if you must know. Not that it's any of your business.'

Since they'd fought, Becca usually ignored her, or made catty remarks. And by the way Becca's eyes suddenly went narrow, Nell knew one was heading her way, right this moment. 'Anyway, who invited you? Gwen never said you were coming. Didn't think parties were your thing.'

'I changed my mind.'

She held up tortilla chips and a four-pack of energy drinks. Becca grabbed one and began to gulp it down, forgetting about her as the next lot of arrivals hammered on the door.

Good. Nell only wanted to look around. She wasn't here to party. An image flitted into her mind, of the Elven on their sledges looking so scared as their world crumbled about them. She was here to check out emergency accommodation for Elven refugees. The main room was big enough, and there were cushions, beanbags and a couple of sofas round the walls. A wood-burning stove with a long metal pipe going up through the roof was blasting out heat. They would be warm and safe here.

There was no electricity of course. Everyone must have raided their parents' sheds for portable lanterns and camping lights. They glowed prettily from every wall and table. Luckily the windows at the front were boarded up, so no light would spill out and give them away. A boy in the corner was DJing from a laptop attached to speakers balanced on a rickety old table tennis table which was also being used as a bar and snacks table.

Gwen was here, there and everywhere, the white streak down one side of her hair shining brightly – the one souvenir of her trip into the Elven world. She was in her element. Nell watched her dancing round the room, chatting and laughing with everyone. Being with a crowd charged Gwen's batteries. A lone Gwen was a sad, bored Gwen.

Whilst I'm the opposite, she thought. I run down when I'm in a crowd, and then have to charge my batteries by being on my own for a while.

'Hey, little sister!' Gwen had seen her. She slung an arm round her shoulders. 'Sisters hanging together.'

'Yeah,' said Nell and waited for Gwen to get bored and drift away, which she did after a nanosecond.

'Don't touch the punch. It's lethal,' she said, and was gone.

Now to explore the rest of the pavilion. There were three doors, one on either side of the room and one at the back. She tried a side door, and it led to a storage room full of old sports equipment and chairs, plenty of chairs. This was good and useful. She wandered back through the party to the other side door. The handle was broken and the wood warped. She kicked it and it squeaked open. There were rows of pegs and foot lockers. It smelled of damp and old trainers. Changing rooms, definitely. Beyond it was a door labelled 'showers'. Again, good. She wandered in.

A skylight was letting in a few beams of moonlight. This was where everyone had dumped their coats and scarves and woolly hats. That's why she didn't see Jake straight away.

'Nell?'

He was sitting on one of the foot lockers, swigging from a bottle of cider. He was the boy version of Gwen: whatever he wore was cool, and his hair was always cut in the right style. He stared mournfully at her.

'What's up?' she said.

'She dumped me.'

Gwen and Jake had been together since Year 8. The split had been the talk of the school.

'Yeah, I heard.' Nell kicked at the locker. She'd more than heard about it. Gwen had gone on and on about how she felt different after getting lost in the woods. The Elven forest had changed Gwen, even though she couldn't remember it.

Jake took another swig of cider. 'Is she going out with

someone else?'

'No.'

It was true, but it wasn't the whole truth. Nell had seen Gwen doodling on the covers of her school books. It had made her blood run cold, because Gwen was doodling boys – pretty good anime versions of Elven boys. This was something Nell had strictly not allowed herself to do. She didn't want to become the sort of moonstruck girl who was forever drawing the boy she fancied. But Gwen wasn't doodling just any Elven boy, she was mainly doodling Fen. There was no mistaking that wolfish grin, white hair and sly charcoal eyes. Gwen hadn't got immunity to the Elven like she had, but somewhere, somehow, a part of her sister's brain was remembering that dangerous and crazy Elven who'd nearly trapped her in his world. Fen, who might have killed them both, if she and Evan hadn't worked together.

Gwen would draw her little sketches of Fen and then scribble them out so hard the pencil tip broke. It was as though deep down she knew what he'd done and was angry.

'She won't tell me what's up,' he muttered. 'I went round to her house. She wouldn't let me in.'

Nell cringed for him. That had been awful. Jake pleading, Gwen standing there, looking at her nails

40

and hardly acknowledging him. 'Yeah. That was harsh,' she agreed.

Jake jumped as though he'd forgotten she was standing in front of him. He pushed the hair out of his eyes and looked up at her. 'Huh? She told you?'

Nell frowned. 'I was there, Jake, when you called. I answered the door. It's my house, too. Remember?'

'Oh. Right. Whatever.' He stood up, swigged the last of his cider, threw the bottle into one of the lockers and wandered away, as though he'd forgotten about her again after only a few seconds.

This wasn't too much of a surprise to her. She'd never been high visibility at school like Gwen, but it was definitely getting worse. At school, if she wanted to be left alone in a lesson, she would find that even the teachers would forget she was there. Was she slipping away from this world, because she was thinking about the Elven world so often? Would she end up falling between the two, and belonging to neither of them?

Or maybe she was learning how to charm like the Elven.

She followed Jake back into the party room. Gwen was darting about the place, counting heads.

'Twenty-three, twenty-four, twenty-five. We're all here. Lock the door, Becks. We don't want gatecrashers.'

Becca turned the key.

'Wait.' Nell made for the door. Now she'd checked out the pavilion, she could go home. 'Let me out first.'

As she reached the door someone tapped on it. No, not tapped, more like ran their fingernails down the icy, splintered wood. *Scritch, scritch, scritch.*

'Go away,' shouted Gwen. 'Find your own party.'

'Aha. I have an invite,' called a voice.

Nell stopped dead. It was a voice like Evan's. But it couldn't be him. It wasn't him. The accent was nearly Elven, but there was something different about it, it was not as singsong, and it was more . . . more – dangerous?

'Hey. Let me in!'

Her heart did one of its worrying big beats and then lots of fast ones. Her fingers went to her pulse. She hadn't done that since she'd got back from the Elven forest, but that voice *scritch, scritch, scritch*ed worryingly on her brain.

It didn't worry Becca. She gave a squeal and came alive. She tucked a stray lock of hair behind her ear, pulled her raggedy ponytail tighter, pushed Nell out of the way and swung the door open.

Nell stared in confusion at the boy who stood there.

Elven! No, not Elven.

He looked about her age or a little older. He was

wearing shades of grey. Against the black sky he shone out. His grey hoodie was not even done up against the freezing wind. The sleeves were pushed back up his arms. His shiny hair was blowing like raven feathers, his smile super-friendly as he looked at Becca and at Gwen beside her.

'Yum, yum,' whispered a girl behind her.

Nell shrank back. She wanted to run. She didn't trust that friendly face one little bit. But any movement would attract attention.

You're not human, you're not Elven, she thought wildly. What are you?

'Let him in, Becca,' said another girl, happily. 'He must be freezing.'

Suddenly Nell didn't care if he saw her.

'No. He can't come in. He's not invited.'

Becca whirled round at her. Everyone else stared, scenting trouble. The noise of the party dropped as though the volume control had been turned down. The music track finished but the DJ didn't notice.

'Shut up. It's not your party,' said Becca, in a threatening voice. Then she beamed at the boy. 'Hey, you came!'

Nell pushed forward and put her hand across the door. 'No! Everyone's here. The party's full.'

She didn't look at him. She concentrated on Becca,

whose mouth dropped open in surprise and then went all mean and twisted. She thumped Nell's arm.

'I say he can come in, so just shut up.'

But Gwen sprang to her side, her eyes fixed on the new boy, who was standing and grinning as though he was enjoying being fought over. 'She's right, Becks. We don't know him.'

Did Gwen feel it, too? That this boy was a threat.

Becca looked baffled. 'So? I invited him. I know him. He's Loki.'

'How come Gwen doesn't know him?' said Nell. 'Where did you meet him?'

'None of your business.' Becca pushed her aside. She opened the door wider. 'Come on in. Ignore her.'

There was nothing more Nell could do. She stepped back as he came in.

'Wait,' he said, as Becca moved to close the door. It was as though he'd given her a command. She stopped as still as a statue, the door still open. 'My sister can come in as well.'

Before Nell could say anything, a girl flaunted through the door and stepped into the room, all long graceful legs like Bambi. 'Hi!'

If the party had gone quiet before, now it was totally silent.

'Whoa!' said Jake, standing up from a beanbag as though he was on hydraulics.

Nell gawped at the girl along with everyone else. She was the same height as her brother, with the same colouring, the same face, cute and sly both together. She had the same black hair, but longer. If a raven could have feathers as long as a bird of paradise, then they would look like this, and blow in the icy wind like this. Her face looked as though it had been air-brushed in snow.

'I'm Laki,' the girl said, with a dazzling smile.

Nell immediately knew she was as dangerous as her brother. Maybe more so. She looked like a young cat that's just seen a room full of fun mice. She even licked her lips as though hungry for the kill. But that didn't stop Nell wanting to look like her and dress like her. She was in shades of grey the same as her brother. But her grey outfit consisted of shorts and a top that didn't meet in the middle. Her legs were bare until her small boots with a little heel. It was minus eight tonight, maybe lower, and she was dressed for a summer's day. Usually it was Gwen and her gang who looked underdressed, but tonight even they were in jumpers and leggings. Now it was the new girl, brushing snow off her white arms as though it was sand and she was at the beach.

'Told you,' muttered the girl behind Nell to a friend.

'Fake bake is over. I want to be pale like her.'

Gwen stared. Nell could tell something about them was bugging her. 'Yeah, Loki and Laki,' she muttered. 'Cute. Like twins.'

'Want a drink?' said Jake, almost pushing Nell out of the way to get to Laki.

'No. Not thirsty.' She ran her hand through her hair. A ring on her finger caught the light and sparkled. It was curled round like a snake, with rubies for eyes. Nell recognized it. She'd seen it before, when visiting Becca's shop with Gwen in the past. Everyone knew it had been stolen.

Jake hadn't noticed. 'You're foreign. Are you exchange students?' he was saying. 'Are you going to be at our school when we start back?'

'No. Don't think so.'

Nell nudged Gwen, who was still staring from Loki to Laki and frowning. 'Look at her ring.'

'Oh. Jeez, you're right!' Gwen swung into action. She grabbed Laki's hand and held it up. 'Hey, Becca,' she said loudly. 'Isn't this your dad's—'

She got no farther. The girl narrowed her eyes and said, 'Loki, deal with it.'

He touched Gwen's arm. 'No, it isn't the same. It's different.'

46

'What?' Gwen blinked. 'Oh. Yeah. Of course.'

Nell glanced around. Everyone had accepted this. Only she remembered the truth. She turned back. Two identical pairs of silvery eyes were staring straight at her. Laki's with laughing curiosity. And Loki's dangerously. He smiled at her.

I bet everyone, especially Becca, thinks that smile is cute, she thought. Can no one but me see that it's more like a snarl?

It was Becca who broke the staring contest.

'Come and meet our gang,' she said, wrapping her arms round Loki's arm and trying to drag him away. He didn't move.

'Leave me.'

Becca let go of him as though he'd stung her.

'Nell,' he said. 'She's the one I want to talk to.'

Becca's face was a picture. 'Later. Come and meet—'

He waved a hand and Becca wilted. It was like seeing a puppet whose strings had been loosened.

Then he glanced around and touched a few people on the arm. 'Forget me.'

Everyone forgot about him. They began buzzing round Laki, whilst she tossed her hair about and cheeked everyone and had an answer ready for whatever was said.

Nell began to shiver, not from the cold but because she

felt danger. Like an animal sensing a predator, she was getting ready to run. Yes, a predator, that's what he was. She'd made it obvious she didn't want anything to do with Loki, but he was determined to pursue her. She had to get out of here, fast. She faded into the shadows at the back of the room, as everyone else pushed forward. Gwen and Becca's parties were generally dark affairs, but this was where the shadows were the deepest. She kept going until her back hit the door. She fumbled for the handle. Too late. Suddenly her breath became an ice cloud. The temperature around her had dropped in a split second.

Loki was close beside her, radiating cold. He smelled of ice and snow, even in this hot room. But not of pine needles, like Evan.

'Go away. I don't want to talk to you.' She felt in her pocket, trying not to let him notice. Maybe she had something made of steel or iron on her, and she could ward him off, like vampires shrink from garlic. But there was nothing.

In any case he didn't exactly look as threatening as a vampire now, even she had to admit. He was nibbling on a biscuit from the snacks table, and seemed more interested in getting a sugar hit.

'Why do you want to talk to me?' she said. Ice was

warmer than her voice. He couldn't fail to notice. He did.

He gave a little laugh. 'You're the most interesting girl in this whole room, of course.'

'No I'm not. That's stupid. Go talk to Becca. She thinks you're fascinating.'

She saw him try to hide a stab of annoyance. Probably boys this cute looking didn't often get told to go away.

'Most people find me fascinating,' he said, like he had armour against put-downs. 'I usually win them over.'

She met his eyes squarely. 'Not me. Your charm won't work on me. I'm immune.'

She moved away from the door, hoping he wouldn't follow, but there was a blur and he was in front of her again.

'Aha.' Still that smile. 'I'm hurt. Why are you ignoring me, Nell?'

She took a deep breath and told herself to stay calm, even though he was achieving the clever trick of scaring her and getting on her nerves at the same time. Whatever power he had was making her twitchier than two mugs of her mum's hot java lava coffee.

'OK. Your sister's wearing the stolen ring from Becca's shop. Doesn't take much to think you're the thief. It got Becca into loads of trouble,' she said, forcing herself to keep eye contact with him. 'And she's acting really weird. Like you've put some sort of hex on her.'

He gave a laugh. 'It was easy.'

Now he'd annoyed her. She never thought she'd see herself sticking up for Gwen's best friend, but she had no choice. 'Becca's bitchy and silly, but she's not bad. I saw you brush her aside. You treated her like she was nothing, just someone to get you into this party.'

Unbelievably, he treated that like a compliment. He moved closer. 'She is nothing. She's not you.'

'That's a stupid thing to say. Of course she isn't. No one is me, but me.' She knew she was babbling, but he was standing too close and she couldn't move because there was the drinks table behind her and too many people either side. Anyway she didn't see why she should. He should be the one to back off. To help him along, she put her hand out and pushed him.

'Leave me alone,' she said.

'Hey!' said a cheerful voice. 'Is my brother being a pain?' It was Laki, hands in her pockets, her eyes twinkling at Nell.

'Yes, he is.' Nell didn't smile back. She didn't trust either of them.

Loki pretended to look upset. 'Nell doesn't like us.'

'She's clever for a human,' said Laki, looking Nell up

and down, and apparently liking what she saw. 'She's cleverer than you, Loki.' She wrinkled her nose and smiled at Nell. 'But she'll like me. I'll be her friend. It'll be fun having a human friend.'

'Never.' Nell raised her chin. 'I know what you both are.'

Loki laughed. 'I don't think you do.'

She gave him one last Gwen-type withering look. 'Want to bet?'

She turned and walked off. One glance over her shoulder told her they hadn't followed. She quickly pushed the back door open and slipped through. She found herself in a boathouse. The windows weren't boarded up here, and the moonlight was streaming in through the cobwebbed glass. It illuminated a big storeroom. Against the walls were racks holding old mouldy canoes. In front of her was a big sliding door. It was wide open and led to the frozen river. In the moonlight it looked like a band of silver.

She walked outside and stood on the packed ice and snow on the quayside above the river. A few of Jake's mates were messing around out there. They were sliding down the icy boat ramp, daring each other to step on the frozen water.

'Don't. It's not thick enough,' she called to them.

She couldn't help herself, she didn't like ice-covered rivers or ponds.

'It's been minus ten, it's like Siberia,' one of them yelled back. 'Course it's thick enough. So – duh, Nell.'

But she couldn't let it drop. Anyway, it was making her forget about Loki. 'It's fast running. Fast running streams don't freeze well,' she told them. 'It's not a pond. It'll pull you under.' She shivered at the thought. She always imagined the ice breaking beneath her feet and slipping under, and not being able to get to the surface. Or worse still, floating away from the hole, then coming up and finding ice above her.

To prove a point, one of the boys hurled a branch. It twanged off the ice and bounced a couple of times. 'See, Nell. You don't know everything.'

'Hey, let's try this!' One of the boys came staggering back with a breeze block that had been keeping the door open. He heaved it over the side. There was a moment's silence, then a thud and a loud crack. The ice shattered and the block disappeared.

Nell pulled her sleeves over her hands and shivered at the sight of the rushing black water beneath.

'See. Told you.'

'Yeah, whatever,' said the thrower.

Muttering to themselves, the boys wandered off. Nell

stayed on the edge of the quay. Ahead of her, over the white roofs of the houses and past the spire of the church, she could just make out the tops of the trees in the wood.

How long will it take you, Evan, to get here. Can you flit? Did you hear? Do you know your way back?

Thinking about Evan banished Loki's sly face from her mind at last. She was about to go home when she heard footsteps coming up fast behind her. She glanced over her shoulder. It was Becca. Her face was all twisted with anger. She ran straight at Nell, her hands out in front like a battering ram. Nell had no time to move. She felt Becca's hands smack into her back. Her feet slipped and she skidded off the edge of the quay and fell face first towards the frozen river.

Four

Nell swung in midair. Something or someone was holding the back of her coat. Her hands and feet had smashed through the ice, and they were freezing. Her toes were going numb as the water seeped through her boots. She was hauled up to the quayside like a sack of spuds, and there she could do nothing but crouch and try to stop her mind freaking out.

She'd nearly crashed through the ice! It was her nightmare. Her mind skittered about at hyper-speed, imagining slipping under as the current took hold of her, and staring up at ice above, knocking desperately on it as she slid along, seeing the world as a blur and unable to get to it. But at last she managed to calm her breathing and actually look up and see who'd rescued her.

A face was peering down. Charcoal eyes, darker than any she'd ever seen on a human. And a face wide at the cheeks and pointed at the chin, as pale as the snow around them. It was topped by a shock of white hair and framed by a hood thrown back and edged with some kind of fur. It was the one face she'd never expected to see so quickly. The one face that made her heart race, even though it was already going too fast from the fright of falling into the ice.

'You're safe. I caught you, Nell.'

Evan, back from the edge of beyond, just when she needed him. That happened in books, not in real life, but there he was. His hand was still on her arm, she could feel the warmth coming through her coat.

'You?' she managed.

He gave his tricky smile. It was *almost* the same as she remembered – and she remembered everything about him. 'Yep. Saved you. Again.'

She scrambled to her feet. What she really wanted to do was cry out in relief and throw her arms around his neck, like Gwen would. She wanted to hug him, and sigh with relief that he was still alive and out of danger now. That's what she wanted to do, because they had a bond, hadn't they? Something special had happened between them, even though they were Elven and human.

But she held back, and somehow the hug and her joy

at seeing him got translated into an embarrassed smile and a sarky comment.

'My feet got wet. You could've got here a bit quicker.'

Stupid thing to say! His twisty grin stayed but she could tell he was feeling awkward, too. He took hold of her scarf, which had dipped its ends in the river and was now dripping icy water down her coat, and unravelled it from her neck.

'You don't fool me. You're awed, I can tell.' He dropped the scarf to the ground. 'I flit from halfway round the world and I catch you just in time.'

'Very clever.'

The joking was the same, the smile was almost the same, but right from the start Nell could feel that something was wrong. He reminded her of his wolf, Faolan. Behind the friendliness he was watchful and on guard.

A wail from Becca made them both jump. She was sitting on the snow and staring daggers at Evan.

'You pushed me.' Her lip quivered like a baby's.

Had she already forgotten what she'd done?

Evan gave a little snarl. 'Because you pushed Nell.'

Becca's lip quivered even more. 'I don't know what you're talking about. Who are you anyway?' Tears started to stream down her cheeks. 'Why am I out here?'

Any moment now she would start screaming.

'Do your charm thing, quickly,' began Nell, but he was already on his way over to Becca.

He pulled her to her feet. The sound of bees began to buzz around him and then around Becca. It was two months since she'd heard that Elven trick, the buzzing that got into the brains of humans who weren't immune to them. The one that put a block in their brains and made them forget they ever saw a pale boy with white hair and eyes like charcoal.

Nell watched Becca and saw her relax and forget about Evan. And forget about his friend, also. The one in combats, who was standing farther away with a scowl on his face, and hair so long that if he went to her school, he'd fit in with the indie kids.

As Becca gave a sigh and wandered back indoors, Nell said, 'Hi, Falcon.'

The boy mumbled a greeting. Out of all the Elven, he'd been the most distrustful of humans. She expected it from him, but not from Evan.

'You got my message?' she said as he came back.

'Hard not to, really. The wolves went crazy.' He paused and seemed to remember what she'd done. 'Thanks. Star's in awe of you.'

Well, that was something. 'You got here pretty quick.'

He shrugged. 'We flitted.'

She couldn't stand it any longer. 'What's up?'

He rubbed his eyes. 'Sorry. We're tired. We need food. We've never flitted for so long.'

Maybe that's all it was. They'd travelled a long way and they were exhausted. But she wasn't so sure.

'I bet they were pleased to see you,' she said, rubbing her freezing hands.

He nodded. He moved out of the shadows and she got a good look at him for the first time. His hair had grown longer. He looked fiercer and wilder than before.

What did she expect? He'd been in Siberia, living outside with wolves.

Both he and Falcon wore clothes she'd never seen before, hooded and lined with soft fur that looked almost like feathers, and made of some kind of material she'd never seen before. It shimmered and her eyes could hardly focus on it. Most of all it looked warm, she thought enviously. As though reading her thoughts, Evan fished a pair of gloves out of his pocket. They were made of the same stuff.

'Here, have these. You're freezing.'

She took them and put them on. Either she was imagining it, or else the gloves had tiny heaters inside. Her hands began to warm up immediately.

'Elven deep-winter clothes,' he said, noticing her surprise. 'They're made from the feathers of the snow geese that live on the winter lake. You'll never freeze wearing them.'

The music from the party got louder and then quieter again. They ought to move, Nell thought, or someone might come out and see them. Something growled in the shadows.

'Shush, Faolan,' said Evan.

So his wolf was here. She strutted out of the darkness, followed by a second wolf. Another grey like Faolan, but lighter and brindled with a darker grey.

'They must have helped you, in Siberia,' said Nell.

'They guarded us, they hunted for us.' He stopped. Now Faolan began growling. 'Something's wrong.'

'Let's go,' said Falcon. 'I said we shouldn't come here.'

'Wait. I know what it is,' said Nell. 'Did Star tell you that they'd seen Ice Elven?'

Evan was staring into the shadows. 'She told me, but I don't think it can be true. Maybe she saw one of the lone Elven who live on the fringes of the forest.'

'No, she really did see them,' Nell began. But Falcon interrupted.

'The Ice Elven never leave the lake. Star's heard too many stories about how they'll come and get us, with their icy fingers and their stopped hearts.'

Faolan's growls were getting louder and more urgent.

Nell could see a patch of grey against the white snow banked against the side of the pavilion. 'Well, they walk around pretty well for beings with no pulse. There's one here now.'

Loki materialized from the snow like a special effect and walked towards them, grinning. Falcon and Evan swore in surprise and horror. Faolan's fur rose in a ridge down her back. She darted forward, muzzle wrinkled back, teeth showing.

Loki didn't even look at her. He pointed a finger. 'Down, wolf.'

Faolan skidded to a halt, her back paws trying to overtake her front ones, and did a barrel roll as though she'd been hit by a taser. Evan and Falcon drew breaths. They and the wolves had gone very still, as though the arrival of Loki had iced them all.

Two Elven on one side, one Ice Elven facing them. Nell looked from one to the other. White hair and charcoal eyes, opposite black hair and silver eyes. Their faces so similar, but Loki's expression was dangerous and sly.

'Loki and Laki. His sister's inside,' she said. 'They gatecrashed the party. And now everyone likes them.'

Evan made a hissing sound, like a snake. 'So Star was

right. Ice Elven.' There was alarm as well as anger in his voice, but he was trying to hide it. 'Loki what? Stone or Thorn?'

Loki gave a smug smile. 'Thorn, of course. The best.'

Nell remembered the Elven history Evan had told her. The whole Elven race consisted of ten great-families. Eight stayed in the forest. Two went to the Ice. The Stones and the Thorns.

'Now I understand why Becca attacked Nell,' said Evan, glaring at Loki. 'Which one of you tranced her, you or your sister?'

Loki put his hand up, like he was answering a question at school. 'Me. Sorry.' He smiled at Nell and wrinkled his nose. He wasn't sorry at all.

'Tranced?' she said. 'What's that mean?'

Loki pulled what he probably thought was a modest face. 'Aha, we're more talented than the Forest Elven. They can charm you, make you forget about them, do a few hexes, make you sleep, that sort of thing. We can make you do whatever we want.'

'So you made Becca push me?'

Loki looked pleased with himself. 'It was a trial. I wanted to see what I could get her to do. I knew you wouldn't die or anything.'

Nell really wanted to slap him now. To wipe away that

sly smile. 'How could you know that?'

'I know about ice. You got scared for nothing.' He tried to look concerned, but that didn't work either. 'You should see where we live, on the winter lake. That goes down and down and . . .'

She tried to hide her shudder. The thought of bottomless black water beneath the ice, just waiting to sweep her away . . .

'No thanks.'

He's like a cat, she thought, he doesn't even think there's anything wrong with playing around with us, because it pleases him. And that's all that matters.

'It wasn't hard to trance the human girl,' said Loki, prowling up to Evan and circling him, looking him up and down. 'She was jealous of Nell, anyway. Silly humans.'

Loki looked like he'd never be jealous, because he'd never believe anyone was better than himself.

Evan spun on his heel, keeping him in sight. Falcon was still staring as though he couldn't believe his eyes.

'What do you want with us?' said Evan.

Loki stopped. 'You're famous. An Elven and a human making friends. Helping each other. We wanted to meet you.'

'Ice Elven don't like Forest Elven. And you hate

humans. You're lying. Why are you here?'

Loki gave a sigh, as though he'd been found out. It was all acting, he didn't care what he told them, lies or truth. 'We came to get some of our gold back. And have a look at the human world.' He grinned. 'It's fun. Laki loves it.'

'Really?' said Evan. 'Sightseeing while the harps are stopping.'

He shrugged. 'We're not worried about the harps. Ice Elven have plans.'

'To come and live in our world?' said Nell.

Loki pretended to shudder. 'Urgh. No thanks. We hate you. But you're fun to play around with.' His face did a rapid change to slyly happy. 'Your sister and her friends really like us now. They're in our power.'

That did it. Nell snapped. She stormed over and thumped him in the chest.

'You harm my sister or any of her friends, or charm them, or . . . or trance them, and I'll . . . I'll . . . I'll lock you in a sauna, I swear I will. I'll build a big fire and thaw you out. Both of you.'

A shadow moved and a door banged. Someone else was coming outside.

'Loki?' It was his sister, skipping down the icy ramp without a single slip. 'What's going on?'

Nell heard Evan and Falcon give a gasp as they saw Laki.

The Ice Elven girl gave a giggle. 'And who's going to thaw us out?'

'Me.' Nell turned away. 'Are you coming?' she said to Evan and Falcon.

Without waiting for an answer she walked off across the frozen playing fields, slipping and sliding and wanting to kick something in anger. After a few moments they caught up with her.

'Where are you going?' Evan said, suspiciously.

She stopped. 'To hand you over to the bosses of the Watchers. Where else?'

Falcon swore, but Evan said, 'Very funny.'

She looked at their weary, tetchy faces and her anger subsided. 'You said you were hungry. I'm inviting you back to my place.'

She was amazed with the way her voice came out calm and steady as though she often had boys back to her house.

But please don't let Mum be back, she prayed.

They were sitting on her bed, as she balanced in with the tray. There wasn't anywhere else for them to sit, the room wasn't exactly big or tidy. If she'd known she might have company she'd have put the books back on her shelves, tidied up the pile of mags and done something about the chair heaped with discarded clothes.

There's two Elven boys in my room, she thought as she set the tray down on her bedside table, and I'm worrying about it being tidy? Anyway, they're boys, they won't notice.

Falcon was already half asleep. Evan was cross-legged, a stack of pillows behind him.

'Comfort,' he said. He'd relaxed his guard since coming inside. 'And hot drinks.'

The wolves had been sent back to wait by the mist, disappearing into the night, their tails low as though they were being punished. She might just get away with two boys, if her mum came back unexpectedly, but two wolves? Never.

She handed them a mug each. 'Hot chocolate. It's my signature drink.'

They warmed their hands round the mugs and started to sip. They sipped and breathed out clouds of steam, and sipped and sighed. Then they saw the plate of biscuits. Falcon sniffed a Jaffa Cake like a little wolf. Then ate it in one bite.

Maybe this was their first hot drink for two months, Nell thought. Could a human boy or girl have spent that long in the wilderness, with only a wolf to hunt for them? Not anyone she knew, for sure.

She wasn't surprised, a few minutes later, when Falcon yawned and then closed his eyes. They looked like they hadn't slept for days. She went and sat on the bed beside Evan.

'I can't get the Ice Elven out of my mind,' she said with a shiver. 'Do you think they would move to this world?'

'No. Never. They hate it here.' Evan looked out of the window where icicles framed the snowy garden. 'They couldn't live in this weather.'

'But they're Ice Elven,' she said. 'I thought they liked the cold.'

'They do. They live on the winter lake. It makes this seem like a tropical island. It would make Siberia seem friendly.'

'How can they survive, then?'

'The stories say their hearts don't beat,' said Evan. 'But they do, about once a month. Even their blood is nearly ice.'

'So why are they here?'

'I don't know. But I'll find out. Stay clear of them, though. And Becca.'

Falcon was fast asleep now. She sat back and hugged her knees.

'I don't want to talk about Ice Elven any more. Tell me what happened at the camp.'

At first she thought he wasn't going to tell her. His face went guarded again.

'It was terrible,' he said, eventually. 'It's changed me.'

Nell shivered. She was right. There was something different about him.

'When Star took me through the Siberian mist, I couldn't believe you'd ever find a small camp in amongst all those mountains and that wilderness,' she said.

She saw shadows start to move on his face, like last time when he'd told her about his family in the iron camp. This time, as he told her how cold they'd become, and how they'd walked for days, hardly sleeping, snow formed on his eyelashes and frost on his face.

'We had human devices, satnavs and the co-ordinates. But best of all we had Elven devices. Wolf noses. Even so the camp turned out to be miles and miles away. We made lots of wrong turns, so it took us days that first time, even with flitting.'

He paused, and a network of scratches criss-crossed his face now.

'Birds attacked us,' he muttered. 'Buzzards. They were hungry. Starving. They thought we were prey. As soon as we got near the camp, though, we smelled the iron.

68

It stank. It choked us. Imagine the Elven – they have to live with that all the time.'

More shadows moved on his face.

'And it was booby-trapped with iron. Falcon walked into one trap, a circle of iron that snapped shut around his leg. Luckily I missed it, so I found a stick and got him free. We had to tread carefully after that. But when we got nearer there was some kind of device that was like invisible iron, that sent us dizzy.'

Nell frowned. 'Something magnetic maybe? A device that puts an invisible field around the camp.'

'Uh-huh. Even if we could have blown up the iron fence from a distance, they still couldn't escape.'

He took a mobile phone from his pocket and clicked a few times, then held it out to her.

This was an outside view of the place she'd seen on Dru's webcam.

'It's bigger than I thought,' she said. And bleaker.

'They're expanding it. There's Elven children who were born there, so they're building more schools. We watched them. There were so many guards. It's like a little town. They'll never let the Elven free, not if they're making schools.'

Evan looked so distraught that she felt heartbroken for him and Falcon.

'Star said you tried everything.'

He held out his hands. They were covered in scratches and cuts.

'We've been trying to dig tunnels.'

'In frozen soil?'

'We found a fox hole that went deep and headed towards the camp. We hollowed it out at night. We thawed it as we went. We lived in it.' Suddenly he looked tired and worn out. 'We've been like foxes ourselves, hibernating underground.'

She could smell the earth on him, but he still smelled of pines, Elven always smelled of pine. And now she knew that Ice Elven smelled of snow.

'Did you see your mum and dad?'

'Yes.' He flicked the phone to another image. 'From far away. We wanted to shout. We wanted to run to them. But we couldn't. They move around. They look tired. The guards don't bother them.' He held the phone out again. It was taken on telephoto and fuzzy. There was a man carrying a small girl with white hair sticking straight up in a whoosh.

'Your little sister?'

'Duck.' He touched the photo. 'Elskling.'

She knew that was an Elven word that meant *precious one*. Evan had said it to her once.

70

'I have to get them out.' He put the phone away. 'Especially now the harps are stopping. Or we'll all end up behind fences ten metres high and chained in iron for ever,' he said, bitterly. 'Now I've seen the camps, I don't trust any human.'

Not even me? she thought. Is that what had changed? He'd become like Falcon and he distrusted everyone.

'But first you have to make Star and the little ones safe,' she reminded him. 'You have to bring them to this world, in case the harps suddenly stop. The pavilion is warm and dry.'

'Yes, but I'd rather save our world than run from it.'

'How? You said no one knows how to mend the harps.'

'Only the Vanir. They're Elven, but they're our gods, too. They made our world, but no one knows where they are now. They disappeared or died a long time ago.'

'Did they write down how they started them?' she said. 'If they did, then maybe you could restart them.'

He frowned. 'The sagas tell how the world began,' he said. 'Maybe they give details of how they did it.'

This seemed more hopeful. 'What are the sagas?'

'Sort of half poem, half story. But they're also our history. Our parents knew them off by heart, but we don't. We've never learned them. They're written down in books, but we don't have any copies.' He yawned. 'Maybe they got stolen by humans.'

Nell sat up. 'Maybe you're right. My nan has shelves of old books. I bet the Watchers would have copies. Let's go and ask her—'

That woke him up. 'No,' he said, roughly. 'I told you. I can't trust anyone. Especially not a Watcher. Can you take them without her knowing?'

'Steal them? No. They're locked up. They're probably worth a lot of money. But don't worry. She's not going to hand you over to her boss. I'll call her and say I need to borrow them. That's not dangerous.'

He didn't look too happy about it, but he looked too weary to argue. 'I suppose I have to risk it.' He yawned again. 'And I don't have a better plan.'

Nell stood up. 'I'll go and call her.'

She ran downstairs and found the phone. When she called Dru's mobile she got the answerphone. She left a message and went back upstairs to find Evan fast asleep beside Falcon. She found a blanket and put it over both of them. Then she dragged Gwen's quilt from the next room and curled up beside them on the bed.

She didn't think she'd be able to sleep but she did, and woke when it was starting to get light. She couldn't think what had disturbed her, then she heard the sound of a car being parked badly outside so that the tyres squeaked on the kerb. A few moments later the front door opened.

'That's it! Two days off,' shouted a voice. 'About blimmin' time!'

Her mum was home.

Five

Footsteps started up the stairs. 'Nell? You awake?'

Nell shot off the bed, throwing the quilt to the floor. She squeezed out of the door and pulled it closed behind her. Jackie was a metre away, kicking discarded clothes into a pile and then scooping them up. She looked exhausted, her hair straggling from her work ponytail, her uniform crumpled.

Nell tried to radiate innocence. 'Yey, Mum! You're home.'

Jackie immediately stopped gathering the washing and looked her up and down. 'What have you done?'

'Me? Nothing.' Nell ran and hugged her. 'I'm happy you're back.' She had to get her mum downstairs. 'Now we can have cooked breakfast!'

'Yes, we can.' Jackie unwrapped herself. 'First – out of my way. I need to get your washing. Otherwise we'll all have nothing to wear.' She tried to push by, but Nell stood firm.

'Leave it, Mum. I'll get it later.' She put her hands together as if praying. 'Breakfast first please, or I'll die of starvation. Gwen and her friends ate all the food you left.'

Jackie frowned at her suspiciously. 'What's wrong with your room?'

Nell tried for another innocent look. 'Nothing.'

Except for two Elven boys sprawled out fast asleep, so they can't make you forget them. And you'll make a fuss, and it will be embarrassing, because Gwen always has boys stopping round in her room, but not me. And you'll want to know who they are.

'Um. It needs tidying.' She grabbed some of the clothes falling from Jackie's tired arms. 'Seriously, Mum – we both need food. We can have egg muffins with red sauce and plastic cheese. Please?'

That stopped Jackie. 'You're right. Muffins. At last I've time to make breakfast, and what do I do? I collect washing when we need food.' She yawned and trailed off down the stairs, dropping Gwen's socks behind her.

Nell's relieved breath puffed out her cheeks. She took a quick glance back into her room. Evan and Falcon were two shocks of white hair wrapped in a blanket. They were sleeping as though they'd been cursed by fairies to sleep for a hundred years.

Please stay quiet, she pleaded silently, as she followed her mum down and ran straight into Gwen. Her sister had crept through the front door moments earlier and was wandering up the hall looking bleary-eyed. The snow party was over. She blinked suspiciously at Nell.

'What happened to you? You just disappeared.'

'A few people were going home so I walked with them.'

Gwen pushed grumpily by her and started kicking her boots off and unwrapping her scarf. 'Tell me next time.'

This was new. Ever since getting lost, Gwen had started to worry about her more. Maybe her sister's world-view now involved someone other than herself.

She certainly looks antsy about something, Nell thought, as Gwen peeled her coat off. Then she found out.

'There's something wrong with Becca,' her sister said. 'Did she say anything to you?'

'No.' She tried to push me into a frozen river though.

Gwen looked puzzled. 'She's acting totally weird.'

'Maybe her dad's getting at her about the break-in.' Or it's because she's been tranced by an Ice Elven, she added silently.

Gwen suddenly snapped out of her after-party vagueness and did one of her super-sharp focuses on Nell.

'What's up? What aren't you telling me?'

Jeez, thought Nell. What's with my family seeing straight through me all of a sudden? She managed a smile. 'Nothing. Mum's cooking egg muffins, though.'

Gwen's face went dreamy. She clutched her stomach. 'Oh. My. God. I'm now officially starving.' She headed into the kitchen. 'Feed me, Mumsie!'

Jackie had already got the frying pan on, and the muffins toasting. Nell went to the fridge for the cheese slices. A tired silence reigned except for the spitting of the eggs and Nell cursing as she tried to pick open the cheese wrappers. Soon they were sitting round, eating. When they were revived by the food, Jackie finally focused on her eldest daughter.

'And where were you all night?'

'Party, party, party.'

Since getting lost in the woods, Nell knew her mum had tried to be strict. She'd refused night shifts at work, she'd not let Gwen out of her sight. It had lasted until after Christmas, when both Nell and Jackie had been grateful to see the back of Gwen and her constant moaning about being stifled and bored.

Lightning doesn't strike twice, was Jackie's new philosophy.

Now, she stood up and stretched. 'Well, I've been at

work, work, work. So keep the noise down, do you hear? No friends round today. None at all. Tidy your room. Get rid of these cans and bottles.'

'OK, OK. Let me sleep first,' groaned Gwen, standing up and dropping crumbs everywhere. 'I'm off to bed.'

With that she flounced off up the stairs. Nell nearly dropped her muffin out of fright. This was dangerous. Gwen had no idea about personal space, and barged into Nell's room whenever she felt like it, usually to borrow something. Above their heads, Gwen's feet stomped across the landing. Nell jumped up.

'I'll go, too.'

Jackie pushed her shoulders down. 'Sit. You're all bones. You need to eat and eat. Here.' She passed her a second muffin.

Nell stared at it. How could she eat when she was holding her breath? Above them, Gwen's footsteps banged across the landing again. Nell relaxed. That way was the bathroom.

Gwen's feet thumped to a halt overhead. A door squeaked. Silence. Then a bloodcurdling scream.

'What the—?' said Jackie, almost dropping the frying pan.

Nell bounced up again, stuffing the last of the muffin into her mouth. 'I'll go. She's seen a spider, I bet.' She gulped and held out her hands. 'See, all gone.'

When she dashed upstairs, Gwen was standing at Nell's bedroom door, with a hand on either side of the frame.

'It's cool. It's nothing.' Nell crept towards her. Gwen turned a horror-struck face, eyes diamond-shaped and glittering. She clutched Nell's hand.

'I don't want them here. Who are they?'

Evan and Falcon were sitting up, hair sticking out, blinking in the light and looking round in confusion. Evan tried to stand but staggered and fell to his knees as the blanket tripped him. Gwen leaped back. A tear rolled down her cheek.

'Tell them to go away. Please.'

'Evan!' hissed Nell. 'Make Gwen forget.'

'Trying.' He rubbed his eyes and squinted and frowned. Falcon was being no use. He was staring back at Gwen like a snake. Slowly a buzzing filled the room, and thankfully Gwen flopped back against the door.

'What's going on up here?'

The stairs creaked as Jackie came up. Nell froze. She and Evan stared at each other.

'Go,' she hissed. 'Meet me in an hour, in the street.'

As Jackie strode towards the bedroom, Evan grabbed Falcon by the shoulder and the two Elven faded through the wall. A moment later there was a double thump from the garden below. A quick glance out of the window and Nell saw them fleeing towards the woods at the bottom.

'What's going on?' said Jackie. They were all in her room now. 'What did you scream for, Gwen?'

Nell watched her sister trying to make sense of what just happened. 'I saw ghosts,' she said at last, and burst into tears. 'Freaky boy ghosts.'

'Hmmm.' Jackie stood with her hands on her hips. 'What sort of party was that last night? You better not be doing drugs.'

Gwen's sobs grew louder. 'I don't! I'm not like that!'

Jackie picked up the blanket and the quilt and threw them on to the bed. She hadn't noticed the smell of pine needles. 'Well, if this is the silly frame of mind you come back in, then you won't be going any more.'

Gwen's mouth dropped open, her eyes filled with more tears.

'Great! Thanks, Mum. I've had a fright, OK? And now you're picking on me.'

She stormed out and Jackie followed. Nell listened to the usual going-nowhere argument, and tried to start breathing normally. Then she went through to Gwen's room and took charge.

'Gwen, shut up. There's no ghosts here. You're tired,

that's all, and seeing things.' She turned to her mum. 'And you're tired as well. I'll put the washing on, and I'll load the dishwasher. Go to bed.' She turned her mum round and escorted her out.

It worked.

Jackie swayed. 'Yes. Bed. Be good.'

'Yes, Mum, I will be.'

If being good meant bringing together two people who distrusted each other.

An hour later she and Evan got on the bus going into town. Dru was already on it, sitting at the back. It was empty apart from an old man who was talking to the driver. Most people were staying in because of the snow.

Evan sat on the opposite end of the back seat, away from Dru. Nell could see that he was nervous and it was making him edgy. He hadn't wanted to come, but Dru had insisted. She perched herself on the seat in front and half turned round so she could see both of them.

As the old man sat down and the bus driver was ready to set off, there was a shout from the road. Nell wiped the frosted window with her sleeve. Laki was hurrying towards the bus stop, wearing a red scarf. Nell recognized it. It was her scarf, the hand-knitted-by-Mum scarf that she'd left at the party. Laki must have seen them get on, but before she could reach it, the bus jolted forward and set off along the treacherous icy roads. She carried on running, but she fell farther and farther behind, until she was a smudge of red in the distance.

'So this is the Elven who helped kidnap my granddaughters,' she heard Dru say.

When Nell turned back from the window, Dru and Evan were already scowling at each other.

'Leave it, Nan. It's over.'

Evan flicked Nell a glance. 'I told you this wasn't a good idea.'

The meeting was only a minute old and already it wasn't going well.

'I'll leave it.' Dru pointed a finger at Evan. 'Just as long as he remembers to stop dragging you into trouble.'

Evan scowled. 'Maybe if you stopped locking my people away . . .'

'Please, don't.' Nell looked from one to the other. This was her idea and it had to work. Jeez, no one else had come up with anything. 'Snapping at each other isn't helping.'

Dru sat back. 'You're right.' She tried to give Evan a smile. 'I knew your dad years ago, and his dad, too. Believe it or not, we could be friends back then.'

'That's the past,' muttered Evan.

Nell ignored him and turned to her grandmother. All she had to do was get the books off Dru, and then they could get away. 'Did you look for the earliest Elven sagas, like I asked? Did you bring them with you?'

Please, please, please. So they could get off the bus, and get away from here, before Evan started arguing.

'No.'

Evan stood up. 'I thought so. This is a waste of time. It's probably a trap.'

'Why?' said Nell, desperately, to Dru. 'I rang you. I asked you. You said you would. We *need* the sagas.'

Dru raised an eyebrow. 'I bet you do.'

Nell's heart sank. So her nan *had* recognized the sound of the dying harps.

'The harps are failing, aren't they? The Elven world is dying. In fact it's almost dead,' said Dru.

Nell nodded without looking at Evan.

'If Watchers like Stan Larson knew this they would panic,' Dru continued. 'They would imagine an invasion of all the remaining Elven into our world. And they'd never allow them to move here permanently. They'd order their destruction. They wouldn't even allow the camps.'

Evan's face looked stricken. '*Murderers*. No wonder we hate you. No wonder Fen did what he did.'

Dru leaned forward. 'Fen! You dare mention him? I'd love to have a word with that—'

'Stop. Both of you!' Nell pleaded. The old man had turned round and was watching. And she could see the bus driver looking in his mirror.

Dru sat back. 'OK, OK.' She met Evan's eyes. 'Believe it or not, I want to help you. I know why you want the sagas. You want to see if there are clues to the beginning of the Elven world, when the harps were started. You want to see if you can mend them.'

Evan sat down again. 'Yes.'

'You want that. I want that,' said Dru. 'Most of the more sensible and caring Watchers who deal with Elven would want that.'

'So give us the sagas,' said Evan.

She eyed him. 'What do you know about the beginning of the Elven world?'

He didn't say anything for a moment, then it all came spilling out. 'Hundreds of years ago humans had been causing trouble for us. They'd driven us out to the fringes. So the Vanir made us another world.'

'Ah, the Vanir,' said Dru, clinging on to the back of the seat as the bus swung round a corner and headed for the town centre. 'Skin like marble. Eyes like black sapphire.'

'They were over a thousand years old, and they knew how to harness the power of sound,' continued Evan. 'They made the giant harp devices. And when they started the harps, the music was so powerful that they were able to steal a bit of this world and twist it into another dimension. Then they made gateways in the mist so that we could still come to you.'

But humans couldn't go to their world, Nell knew. Because something about the harps or the music was poison to humans when they returned. It made them old if they stopped longer than a night and day. She shivered. It had nearly happened to her and Gwen. It had been the most terrifying thing she'd ever faced.

'After they made the Elven world the Vanir disappeared. The Elven think it killed them.' Evan looked at Dru. 'But we need to know how to start the harps playing again.'

Nan sighed again. 'Then I have to disappoint you. I spent last night going through all the earliest Elven saga books. There's nothing more than you already know in them. If the way to start the harps was ever written down, it's not in my library.'

Nell could have cried. Why hadn't her nan told them that in the first place? Why bother to meet them?

'But there's something else that might help you.' Dru

looked from one to the other of them. 'I'm not sure I'm doing the right thing here – but there's someone who knows more about the harps.'

Evan leaned forward. 'Who? Tell us.'

Still Dru hesitated. 'I haven't seen her for a long time. I promised I would leave her alone. She wouldn't see any adults, that's for sure.' She looked at Evan. 'You might be able to persuade her.' She looked worried. 'Be careful. I don't know how she'll react. She's . . . unpredictable, at best.'

She took a piece of paper out of her pocket and handed it to Nell. 'This is the address. It's an hour away. They're watching me, so I can't take you. Get the train.'

Nell glanced at the scribbled writing. There was a name. Miss Dawn. And an address. Holy Bones. Holy Bones Lane. It was in the next town.

'Thanks, Nan.'

The bus jolted over a speed bump and slowed down to go up the High Street. The pavements here were crowded with shoppers wrapped in coats and scarves, braving the weather to get to the sales.

'I'll get off here,' said Dru, standing up. 'You carry on to the next stop, then no one will see us together.'

As Dru moved past her, Nell looked out of the window, and a flash of red in amongst the crowds caught her eye again. Someone was hurrying along the pavement, waving.

'Laki's caught us up!' she exclaimed. 'There she is with my scarf.'

In a flash, Evan was at her side, swaying as the bus lurched over another speed bump. 'Shut up,' he hissed.

Too late.

'Who?' Dru glanced out of the window and caught her breath. Laki was hard to miss as she skipped along, with that black hair, the silvery eyes, the white white skin like it had been powdered with snow.

Dru swore under her breath.

'Ice Elven! I've seen pictures, images. But I've never seen one . . . none of us have . . .' She whirled round to Nell. 'You didn't tell me *they* were here!'

'Is it important?'

Evan pulled at her sleeve. 'Come on. We have to go,' he muttered, urgently.

Too late.

'This changes things.' Dru put a hand on the seat either side, blocking the aisle. 'If the stories are true, the Ice Elven are deadly to humans. They can hold power over us. They can trance us, and make us do things.' She looked at Nell. 'No. You must stay right out of this mess.' Then at Evan. 'Do you hear? My granddaughter is not to give you any more help. Or I'll have to report it.' She stopped and took another look at Laki. 'Maybe I should anyway – this is too big.' She made a snatch for the paper. 'Give me the address back.'

Nell pulled her hand out of the way. 'No.'

Dru made another attempt to grab it.

'Leave her.' Evan's face twisted. He pushed Dru away and dragged Nell to the back of the bus. As the driver braked to avoid a pedestrian, he thumped the emergency door and they leaped down on to the road. Dru's face peered out after them, shouting, but there was nothing she could do to follow them. The bus was already speeding up again.

They ran, dodging and swerving round the shoppers, towards a side street. Down there the crowds were thinner and the shops smaller. It was the start of the old jewellery quarter, and even in the snowy weather there were people window-shopping.

Evan stopped as soon as they were out of sight of the bus. His face was blazing with rage.

'I knew I shouldn't have trusted a Watcher.' He held out his hand. 'Give me the address.'

Nell took a step back, his anger taking her by surprise. 'No. We do this together.'

'You heard your grandmother. She knows about the

Ice Elven and she's scared stiff. She'll tell the other Watchers. They'll hunt us down. So we better stay away from each other.'

She stared at him, open-mouthed. 'What are you saying – we're not friends now? You don't trust me?'

She was right, he had changed. What had happened to that strange and special bond between them, the one that took no notice of the fact that they were human and Elven? Now he was looking at her as though she was one of the enemy too.

'I can't risk it. It's not your people that are going to get exterminated,' he said, bitterly. 'You're not Elven.'

Nell flinched. That stung. *Not Elven*. True, but it shouldn't matter. Not to them. Not after he'd whispered *Elskling* to her, and kissed her. They were special, even Loki said so. But he'd forgotten it all. He was pushing her away – *you're not Elven*. She shoved the address deep in her pocket. 'Tough. We go together or not at all.'

He moved super-fast. He was right beside her.

'Don't make me do this, Nell.'

This close she could see he was scared as well as angry. But it made no difference. He shouldn't be angry at her.

'What're you going to do? Steal it?' she said. 'You could try. I'm not *Elven* but I'm strong.'

He moved so quick she saw nothing but a blur. And he was holding the slip of paper. She grabbed his hand.

'Give it back,' she said.

They stared at each other, hands locked as though they were arm wrestling. We shouldn't be doing this, thought Nell. There's too much at stake to argue and get offended. Maybe he was thinking the same. Maybe he was a split second away from giving his crooked grin and saying, 'Yeah, you're right. I'm sorry. Let's not fight. We're a team. We're famous.'

It didn't happen. Someone shouted her name. As her attention flickered he pulled his hand away and the slip of paper was his.

'This is my problem now,' he said. 'You heard your grandmother. Keep out of it.'

'Hey, Nell!'

Laki was walking towards them. She looked delighted to see Nell. Which was a change from being scowled at.

'Look what I got for you!' she called, waving the scarf.

Evan turned to Nell. 'Don't be fooled by false kindness,' he said urgently. 'Keep away. She's dangerous.'

Suddenly Nell was fed up of being told what to do and think, first by Nan, now by Evan. She was fed up of risking everything to help the Elven, and still being mistrusted.

'She's brought my scarf,' she said, stubbornly. 'What's dangerous about that?'

He scowled at her. 'She's not a friend. Don't be stupid.'

'Don't call me stupid.' She glared right back at him. 'And thanks, but I can look after myself – even though I'm only a *human*.'

She walked off to meet Laki.

Six

'See? I'm not so bad. One scarf returned.'

Laki skipped up to Nell. Everyone else was walking carefully, because the packed snow had a layer of treacherous ice over the top. Laki moved as though she was barefoot on sand, even in her heeled boots. People had stopped to watch her, because she was still wearing the shorts and little top. She unhooked the red scarf from round her neck and wound it twice round Nell's.

'You forgot it last night. I've been looking for you.' Her own neck was bare now.

'Thanks.'

Laki put her head on one side and gave Nell a little kitten look. 'You want to show me round? I'm a stranger, as you know.'

'Um. No thanks. I'm not in the mood.'

Nell carried on walking, resisting the urge to look back

at Evan. The street was lined with jewellery shops, second-hand and new, cheap and expensive. Laki followed her, skipping along at her shoulder and humming to herself.

'Aren't you cold?' said Nell, eventually. She didn't trust Laki one little bit. But that didn't mean there wasn't some part of her that was enjoying having Laki following her. If only to annoy Evan.

'Never. This is nothing.' Laki pretended to fan herself, then she grinned. 'Show me around. Be a good citizen. Find me some fun.'

'Not sure you'll find that much in Woodbridge,' said Nell, trying not to smile in spite of her black mood.

'You'll make it fun,' said Laki. She tried to link arms, as Gwen and her friends always did, but Nell moved away. So Laki walked beside her as they set off into the maze of little streets.

It was like being on stage – everyone looked at Laki, and she wrinkled her nose and laughed back at them. After a while Nell found herself joining in and laughing at the grey, huddled passers-by. They weren't just staring at Laki now, they were staring at her, too, and giving her disapproving looks, as though Laki's dangerous sparkle was rubbing off. For some reason that made her want to laugh, too. Until a thought struck her.

Was Laki trancing her?

Was that why this bubble of fun kept rising up in her, after all the grimness of the meeting with Dru and the argument with Evan?

No, I'm immune, she told herself. Laki couldn't trance her, nor could she charm her. I'm laughing because I want to laugh. Because sometimes when things are earth-shatteringly bad, your mind needs to escape. Especially when people you're trying to help don't trust you any more. Eyes didn't lie. She'd seen the distrust in Evan's eyes.

But just for a moment her sensible self burst through. She stopped in the middle of the street, making several people tut as they swerved round her. Laki raised an eyebrow.

'Problem?'

'What exactly are you and your brother doing here?' Nell asked. 'Besides robbing Becca and then making fun of her?'

Laki flipped her hand as though it was no big deal. 'Oh that? The robbery. That was just us getting some of our family treasures back from humans. One of our uncles was weak of spirit. He left our home to come here.' She pulled an astonished face. 'Can you believe it? How could anyone want to live in this world?'

The astonished face didn't work on Nell. Laki had

been enjoying herself last night, without a doubt. No one was that good at pretending. And she was enjoying herself this morning, walking around the snowy streets, upsetting and shocking people.

'Anything's got to be more exciting than a frozen lake,' Nell said, mock-innocently. 'Even Woodbridge.'

Laki's eyes sparkled. 'Ha. You're sharp. No wonder we've heard so much about you. Truly. You are talked about. You're a celebrity.'

Nell hunched her shoulders with embarrassment, but she couldn't stop the smallest of grins. 'Really?'

'Uh-huh. If I could be friends with anyone here, it would be you.' She tucked her arm through Nell's again. She did it casually, like they were best mates and had known each other for ages. Nell froze. She still didn't trust Laki. She could feel the Ice Elven coldness seeping through her coat. But this time she didn't move away.

Laki squeezed her arm. 'Come shopping with me, Nell. We'll have fun.'

Don't believe her, don't get sucked in, said her sensible brain.

'Why would you want to be friends with me? I think your brother hates humans.'

Laki put her head on one side, silver eyes serious for a moment. 'You're different, I saw it straight away. Loki doesn't like your world. But I'm curious about all this.' She looked around at the shops. 'Most of the adult Ice Elven wouldn't come here. Go near humans? Breathe tainted air?' She did a pretend shudder. 'No, they would hate that.' She giggled. 'But I couldn't wait.' She tugged at Nell's arm. 'Come on. Have a little fun.'

Something gave way in Nell. I don't care if she's trying to trick me, she thought. I don't even care whether she genuinely likes me or not. I'll go with her. I can find out what she and Loki are really doing. I can be as sly and clever as both of them. I can forget that Evan's stormed off and thinks all humans are murderers now.

Anyway, why shouldn't she have a morning away from thinking about the Elven world dying? Why not go round town with a new friend – a new dangerous friend?

I'm always watching, I'm always thinking about things first. But not this time.

'Nell?'

She smiled at Laki. 'Yeah. OK.'

And off they went, Laki holding her up when she skidded, as though they'd been friends for a long time.

I never did that before, thought Nell. Usually it took her ages to be comfortable with someone, before there was that moment when she forgot to be self-conscious with them, and they became a friend. She'd felt that immediate dropping of her guard with Evan, too. It must be an Elven gift. But now he'd shut her out.

'Hey, let's go in here. I want something.'

Laki had stopped and was staring into the window of a small jeweller's specializing in antique pieces. In one corner, sparkling like ice, was a necklace made of gold and some kind of eye-wateringly bright crystal.

Nell hesitated. 'Is it that necklace? What are you going to do?'

Laki's nose was almost on the glass. 'Take back the Thorn jewels. Want to help me?'

Nell burst out laughing. 'Erm. *No*. My mum and dad are in the police.'

Laki laughed back at her. 'This isn't stealing. It's reparation. The reason Uncle Thorn became weak was that he'd tasted human whisky and become addicted. That's why he left the lake. He came to your world and sold our jewels to get more whisky. These jewellers saw he was weak and gave him only a little amount of money. They are the cheaters, now I get revenge.'

Nell knew she should have refused to have anything to do with this. But she didn't. She was way past worry. This was time out from worry. Time out from being sensible.

It was the only way to find out more clues about Laki.

The bell on the door tinkled as she followed Laki

inside. There was a grey-haired man watching them. Before he could say anything, Laki went over and leaned on the counter.

'Hello, sir, can we see the necklace in the window?'

Nell thought he was going to refuse at first, but then he seemed to weaken and he smiled at Laki. 'Of course.'

He came back with it and draped it over his hand to show it off. Even Nell caught her breath. It was amazing, like pure icicles caught on a chain. Side by side, she and Laki admired the necklace.

'Not everyone likes it,' the man said. 'Some people find it unnerving for some reason.'

Laki waved a hand. 'Oh, I see differently to most people,' she assured him. 'More colours, that sort of thing.' She gave him the full blast of her eyes and her smile. It nearly knocked him over.

'There's one problem,' he said kindly, when he'd recovered. 'You'll never be able to afford it.'

'Aha. That's what you think! Can I try it on, please?'

Nell noticed that Laki included a dimple with the smile this time. No one could resist that dimple, certainly not the jeweller. Nell could tell he'd been about to refuse, but instead he smiled back in a dazed fashion and handed it to Laki. She slipped it round her neck. It suited her, her pale skin setting off the lustre of the gold and the iciness of the crystals. Even so Nell's heart was beginning to thump. Maybe there was hidden CCTV.

'Leave it. Let's go,' she whispered. 'This is wrong.'

Laki shook her head. 'Wait. And listen.' She turned to the jeweller. 'Where did you get it?' He stared at her. 'Talk,' she ordered.

He started speaking, reluctantly, but as though he couldn't stop himself.

'It was a couple of years ago. A man came in. He was tall, a hat low over his face, and he was soaked through – it was raining, a terrible night. I only saw his eyes once but they were weird.' He looked away from Laki's silver gaze, as though something was nagging at his mind.

'Forget about silver eyes,' said Laki, quickly.

'He was searching for a buyer, and he'd heard I was a collector.'

'Did he say his name?' Laki murmured.

'Yes. Thorn.'

'You paid him a good price for the necklace?'

The jeweller's face went white and worried. 'He seemed desperate for cash. I checked on the stolen goods database, but it didn't show up. So I gave him a fair price.' He seemed to be trying to keep his mouth closed, but words kept tumbling out.

'A fair price?'

'No! Ridiculous price. I almost stole it from him.' The man clamped his mouth shut. He looked ready to cry. 'He was desperate to sell, that alters things,' he burst out a moment later. 'He seemed happy.' He held out his hand. 'I think I should put it away now.'

'No, you cheated my uncle, because he was drunk. So I get the necklace.'

She leaned over the counter so their faces were close together, their eyes locked.

He gaped like a goldfish and then blinked. 'Oh, OK. I have no objection at all, miss.'

'Thank you!' Laki's dimple reappeared. She looked at the sign on the counter. 'Good doing business with you, Mr S. Stevens, Goldsmith.'

When they were outside on the pavement, Nell thought, Oh my God, I'm part of a robbery, I'm an accessory.

Laki tucked the necklace into her top and patted it. 'So that squares it. Uncle Thorn is avenged.'

Nell shivered and stuck her hands in her pockets. Inside the jeweller's she'd been sweating from fear, and the sweat was now freezing on her face. It looked ready to snow again. Everyone was walking around breathing out their own little ice clouds. Laki linked arms again.

'Poor Nell. You cold? Let's go shopping somewhere

warmer. Let's go have coffee. Show me what you do in your world.' She breathed in deeply. 'I want to know everything before I go back to the lake for good.'

The Oak shopping centre was close by. It was where they always went when they were in town.

'Follow me,' said Nell.

When they walked through the doors into the mall, Laki squeezed her arm with excitement. 'This is good. Let's shop. What sort of things do you like?'

Without realizing, Nell found herself heading towards the row of clothes shops.

'Erm. I like all the different greys you're wearing,' she said, thinking, then I could dye my hair that colour, raven black. Yeah, that would be a good look.

'Grey clothes,' said Laki, looking pleased. 'OK. We get you some.'

Nell stopped. 'I'm not nicking stuff!'

'I've got money. Me and Loki were given plenty of funds. The Ice Elven are richer than you could ever imagine. It'll be my treat, to make up for Loki being bad to you.'

What followed was an amazing hour where they went from shop to shop and Nell collected items for a new outfit. Shop assistants stared at them and followed them round suspiciously. It might have had something to do with Laki picking things off the rails – jackets, hats, scarves, even shoes – then putting them on and walking round in them, close to the doors.

'I'm teasing,' she told Nell. 'I'll pay at the end. I like worrying people that I won't, though.'

They ended up in the coffee bar on the first floor, which was risky because this was where Becca and Gwen hung out. Sure enough as they walked in, arms linked and their hands full of carrier bags, there they were, with Paige and Bria and the rest of their gang. There was a moment's silence – this happened at every place that Laki entered, it seemed – when Gwen and her gang just goggled at them.

Laki beamed round at everyone, then shouted, 'Hey, guys,' to the boys behind the counter. 'We need coffee and cake, right now!'

Soon they were perched on stools at the counter, with their backs to Gwen. Laki read the menu chalked on the wall in front of them. 'What do you like?'

Nell knew she meant food, but instead she said, 'Cats. Wearing dark colours. The sort of blue the sky goes in Cornwall. And daydreaming.' As Laki laughed she added, 'Oh and lemon tart with ice cream.'

They ordered and were soon sitting behind big steaming mugs of coffee and plates of cake. As Nell blew on her coffee to cool it, she could feel Gwen's eyes on her back. She almost laughed. For once she was the fascinating one, the girl who everyone watched with bated breath, and whispered, 'Oh my God, did you see what she just did?' It felt heady. But more importantly, this was her chance to find out a bit more about Laki.

She smiled at the Ice Elven girl. 'So, what do you like?'

Laki put down her mug. 'Um. All ten shades of white. And eating fish.' Nell knew that already. They'd walked by the sushi bar downstairs and Laki had stood at the window licking her lips at the thought of raw fish. 'And I adore reptiles.'

'Seriously?'

'Uh-huh.' Laki smiled fondly, as though she was about to talk about a kitten or a puppy. 'I have a salamander. It lives in the lake, under the ice, but it comes when I call it. I've begged and prayed to Krake not to eat him.'

'Who's Krake?'

For the first time Laki's smile slipped. 'Don't ask. Krake is not a like. He's a hate, but don't tell Loki.' She started eating her cake, and licking the crumbs off her fingers. After a few mouthfuls, she got her smile back again. 'Tell me your hates, Nell.'

Nell had her list ready. 'I hate spiders. And pink. And wearing skirts. And girly girls like my ex-friends.' She glanced over her shoulder at Paige and Bria, who were watching her, and whispering to each other. 'And nasty people. And whispering. When I was little I used to think ghosts were whispering about me on the landing outside my bedroom. Now I can't stand it.' She pushed her empty plate away. 'What else do you hate beside Krake?'

Laki thought about it. 'I hate being told what to do.'

So that meant someone was telling her to do something, something she didn't want to do. She'd told Nell that she wanted to be here in the human world. So maybe it was something she was supposed to do whilst she was here.

Nell shivered, but made herself smile at Laki. 'What else?'

'Just that.'

She put on an innocent expression. 'Evan says the Forest Elven are scared of Ice Elven.'

Laki laughed and licked her fingers for the last time. 'Of course. Everyone should fear us. We respect no one. We're loyal only to ourselves.'

'But what about when the harps stop? You'll have to move here or die.' She didn't add that this was not a good plan, according to her nan.

'Aha. The ice lake will be the last place to dissolve into nothing. We have a little time. We're keeping our options open.' For the first time Laki didn't meet her eyes.

'So what about Evan? What's his plan?'

No way, I'm not telling you anything, Nell thought. She put on a hurt, puzzled look, which wasn't hard. 'I don't know. He's trying to find a way to save your world, of course. But it seems like he's not my friend any more. I'm human so I'm not allowed to know.'

Luckily Laki didn't get the chance to question her any further.

'Nell?'

It was Gwen and Becca, side by side, flicking little glances back and forth at them.

Laki shook her hair back. 'Hey, look, it's the girls from the party. Hi, remember me?' she said to Gwen.

Nell saw a flicker of fear cross her sister's face for a split second. She'd sensed something was wrong, because she'd still got a few memories of the Elven. But she recovered quickly.

'How could we forget?' she said, sarkily. She put a finger up to her temple as though she was thinking. 'Hmm. Now what's your name? Is it Lucky?'

When Gwen got worried she either got tearful or bitchy. That slight stab of fear had sent her into full bitchiness mode.

Laki didn't seem to care. She smiled at Gwen, but it had a hint of shark in it. 'Close. Laki.'

Gwen yawned. 'Whatever.'

Becca was biting her lip and looking like a puppy that's been abandoned. 'Where's Loki?'

Laki collected her bags and slid off the stool. 'Off doing stuff. Fun things.'

Becca stood in her way. 'He was supposed to meet me.'

Laki laughed. 'Boys, huh.' Which made Becca storm back to her seat, looking as though she was going to burst into tears. Laki turned to go, saying to Nell, 'Are you coming?'

'No,' said Gwen. Now it was Gwen standing in Nell's way. 'Come sit with us.'

Nell couldn't stop herself grinning. 'You're inviting me to sit with you? Ha, that's a first!'

Gwen looked peeved. 'Well, I'm saying it now. Say bye to your mate.'

She must be wondering why Laki wants to hang around with me, Nell thought. Then stopped herself. Why shouldn't other girls find her fascinating? Why shouldn't they want to be her friend? She was different. She'd walked in two worlds. She had so many secrets, and knew so much more than anyone else in this café.

Laki was waiting by the door, impatiently tapping the glass with her nails.

'Leave her,' she called to Gwen. 'Nell is special. More

special than any of you. She's known throughout the winter lake.' She clicked her fingers. 'Now – go away.'

And Gwen did, as though she was a little child and had been ordered by a teacher.

When she'd gone, Nell walked out with Laki.

'Known throughout the winter lake. Really?'

Laki shrugged. 'Believe it. You are the human who came into our world and lived. The human who made friends with an Elven.'

Friends with an Elven. Once maybe. Now he'd questioned her trust. And she'd walked off and left him. A worm of guilt moved in her mind. Was he really to blame? His whole world was collapsing. He was out of his mind with worry. Would she have acted any better if it was her world that was threatened?

You've had your time out, she told herself. You've found out what you can from Laki, which is nothing much. Now start worrying about the harps again.

'I've got to go,' she said. And the enormity of the Elven tragedy slammed down on her again. She had to find Evan. She had to convince him to let her help.

They were outside the shopping centre, with the crowds of bargain hunters milling around them.

Laki stopped and put her head on one side. She gave Nell a calculating look, and as though she'd read her mind, said, 'You sweet on Evan?'

Nell felt her cheeks burn. 'We were friends, that's all.'

Laki didn't look convinced at all. She shook her head sadly. 'I like your spirit. But don't bother. Elven and human would never work.' Then she gave Nell a beautiful smile and wrapped her arms round her neck. 'Hug. See you soon.'

When Laki left, Nell stood for a few moments, shoved back and forth by the crowds. She had no idea where to go to find Evan. In the end, for some reason, she trailed after Laki, keeping back and watching where she went, and saw her turn down a side street. Feeling ridiculous, as though she was a kid pretending to be a spy, she peeked round the corner.

Laki was meeting up with Loki. He was sitting on the back of a snow-covered bench, waiting for her. Sitting next to him was Evan.

Dru was already there, when she got home. Whilst her mum was in the kitchen she told her nan the truth. Evan had taken the address from her. He'd left her. He didn't want to know her any more. She had no idea where he was. Dru made her swear it was the truth, and eventually believed her.

As Nell waved her grandmother goodbye she smiled to

herself. She had told Dru the truth, she didn't have the paper any more. But she didn't need it. She'd read the name and address before Evan had snatched it, and she remembered it perfectly.

She looked it up on Google Earth. The small lane was in the old part of the town. There seemed to be only one building, and that was marked as a church. For some reason she shivered. When the satellite photo had been taken all the rest of that area was in sunlight, but Holy Bones Lane and the church were in deep shadow.

Later, as she was sitting on her bed unable to sleep, she heard someone throwing pebbles at her window again. Star? She looked out. No, it was Laki. She crept downstairs. The Ice Elven girl was on the doorstep, beautifully lit by a moonbeam.

'Let me in.'

Nell kept her hands on either side of the door frame. 'No. Mum will hear.'

She really didn't want Laki in her house. Especially not at night. It would be like inviting a tiger inside. It might remain tame, but it might not.

Laki didn't seem that bothered. 'Come outside, then. Let's do something.'

An arctic draught was blowing up the hall and flapping the rugs. Nell pulled the door half closed. 'I can't.'

'OK.' Laki pulled a resigned face as she backed away, her breath clouding in the freezing air. 'But that means the boys are getting all the fun.' She walked off up the path.

Nell swung the door open again. She couldn't resist. 'How?'

Laki turned and grinned. 'Evan's with Loki, robbing your grandmama.'

Seven

By early morning the snow clouds had shifted and the sky was a deep ice blue. A weak sun was shining low across the station platform, causing everything to dazzle. Nell stamped her feet.

If Evan thought he'd got rid of her – he was wrong.

She was wearing her new grey clothes, the red scarf and her Christmas boots. Her ears were freezing, her nose was freezing. She was alone until someone walked out on to the platform moments before the bell rang for the arrival of the train. She put up a hand to shade her eyes.

It was Evan.

She caught her breath. She hadn't expected to see him. Catching a train seemed too slow for an Elven. It was good, though. It meant he wasn't ahead of her.

He'd seen her straight away, but he didn't acknowledge her until he was right there, a step away. Even for an

Elven, he looked white this morning, she thought. Maybe that's what you get when you spend the night thieving from old ladies, instead of sleeping.

'What're you doing here?' he said, scuffing his shoes on the icy ground, not looking at her. Behind him, the train was coming slowly round the bend in the track.

'Same as you. Except I thought you'd flit.'

He gazed over her shoulder now, his eyes narrowed and his mouth turned down in embarrassment or anger. Probably both. 'Too far. Too risky when I don't know the town. I'd steal a car but the roads are snowed under.' He squinted at her. 'Go home.'

'No. I'm getting on the train. I know the address. You can't stop me.'

His eyebrows made an annoyed V. 'I don't want you here.'

That hurt, but she tried not to show it. 'After all we've been through,' she began. He looked away, towards the advancing train. She tried again. 'Did you rob my nan?'

He shrugged. 'Better than waiting to be rounded up and killed.'

She couldn't believe how cold his eyes were, as though they'd never been friends. If it wasn't for the ache in her heart and the sick feeling in her stomach, she could believe she'd dreamed all that.

'Did you get what you were looking for?' she said.

He stared at the train crawling along towards the station. 'Uh-huh.'

'So what was it?'

He didn't answer, but it didn't matter because someone else was hurrying on to the platform, calling and laughing. She knew that laugh. It was like ice shattering. Loki was probably laughing at a dead bird or the old tramp who was slumped on one of the benches.

He walked towards them with his hood up, his black feathery hair peeking out, but the zip still undone, as though he didn't want to risk getting too warm. He looked like he wasn't hurrying, but in a second or two he was right beside her, standing too close, invading her space. Other girls might think he was cute and mysterious, but to her he was just sly and dangerous.

'What did you take from my grandmother's house?'

Loki grinned. 'Just her laptop. We looked up the last number that was called. We rang the camp again.'

Nell looked at Evan. 'Why?'

'He was trying to trance the guard over the phone,' he said. 'He offered to help.'

'It didn't work,' said Loki. He didn't look too gutted by that.

Evan turned to him. 'Listen. Come with me to the

camp. You can stand iron better than us. Look how you got into the Watcher's house. You can undo the gates. We need the adults. One of them might know how to restart the harps.'

Loki managed to look a little downcast. 'Sorry. I can't risk it. My people don't want me helping you. I'd be outcast.'

'But you helped him rob Nan last night,' Nell pointed out. 'You tried to trance the guard – which sounds like a stupid plan, and it didn't work. Yet something sensible like going and opening a gate, you can't do. Funny that.'

She needn't have bothered. Loki looked delighted that he'd got her attention. He gave her a look of mock pity. 'It's an Elven thing, Nell. You can't understand.'

She turned her back on him and spoke only to Evan. 'So you've palled up with him now?' she said. 'Is he coming, too?'

Evan kicked at a chunk of hard ice as the train pulled in behind them and hissed to a halt. It was Loki who answered.

'Yes, I'm looking forward to meeting the mystery person.' He laughed at her dismayed face, as the doors slammed open behind them. 'I wanted to stop a car and trance the driver to take us, but your roads can't handle even this minuscule bit of snow. Laki's so glad, she wants to experience all human life, including trains.'

Before he could say any more, Laki came skipping down the platform as if it was a summer's morning. She was wearing the clothes she'd bought yesterday, and she looked like she'd been clubbing all night. Her top and short skirt were thin and silvery, and glittering in the sun. Her tights were white, her boots furry. All the passengers leaving the train stared at her.

'Hey, Nell!' She kissed her on the cheek. 'Mwaaah! We went to a club last night. You should've come. Humans know how to have fun.' She giggled. 'But now I'm ready for serious stuff. Quick, let's get on. I'm so excited. First time on a train!'

Nell's spirits sank further. 'So you know about it as well?'

'Of course, Evan told us. We're all Elven, Nell.' She wrinkled her nose at Evan. 'Although me and Loki are the *true* ones. Joking!' She squeezed Nell's arm. 'Evan's going to let me and Loki help. Trust us.'

There's no way I trust either of you, she thought as she followed them on to the train. You say you have a plan if the harps stop. That the winter lake won't be affected for a while. That you don't want to move here. But that's not the whole truth. You're up to something.

Loki and Laki weren't the only ones making her nervous, though. As the door slammed behind them

117

and the others pushed into the crowded carriage, she stopped and looked back. Ever since she'd arrived at the station, she'd been convinced that one of the guards was watching her. At one point she'd seen him on his phone, and he'd glanced across at her. Now, as the train lurched and started moving past the station car park, she realized what he'd been up to. Screeching to a halt was the one person who could've stopped her following Evan. Her dad, DI Tom Church.

The way he stormed out of the car, followed by Dru, she knew he was in his Rottweiler mood, determined and ferocious. It used to scare her, but not any more. After Gwen's kidnapping they'd got to know each other a bit better. But he had no love for the Elven, especially Evan. He must have arranged for the station staff to let him know if she or Evan turned up. He'd go crazy now she'd slipped out of his trap.

There was one good thing, though. It meant that her grandmother had confided in her dad. Told him she needed to stop Nell and Evan getting into danger. Which could only mean that they were talking again.

What's faster? she thought. Car or train? She remembered the TV news showing the traffic jams on the county's roads because of the icy conditions.

Train definitely.

* * *

The train was full, standing room only, and very hot after the chill of the platform. Passengers shuffled along and took off their hats and loosened scarves. The air steamed. Loki and Laki were standing farther along the carriage, not holding on, so they swayed and fell about as the train picked up speed. Nell could hear them amusing themselves and annoying the passengers nearest to them by laughing and joking loudly.

She stayed near the door, leaning back on the luggage rack. Evan stood away from her, in the middle, staring out of the window at the white scenery rushing by.

It was an express train and theirs was the first stop. Even so, it seemed to take an age. When the track went close to any roads, Nell found herself furiously checking to see if her father's car was anywhere in sight. Even though the traffic was crawling, she still couldn't relax. Tom had a habit of using his police powers to get him what he wanted. She wouldn't put it past him to order a helicopter.

At last the train started to slow down and people began standing up to collect their bags and coats. This meant Evan had to move closer and closer, until he was right in front of her.

'I can't believe you told them about this,' she said,

trying not to let the hurt show on her face. 'You said you hated the Ice Elven. You said they scared you.'

'They're useful,' he said, quietly but angrily. 'They can withstand iron better than us. They can freeze it and even hold it for a while. I had to take the chance they'd help me.'

Nell glanced at Loki and Laki, but they were too far back to hear. 'But you said they didn't like Forest Elven. Why would they help you?'

Evan's face was stubborn. 'Our world is dying. All Elven have to pull together.'

The train was nearly in the station. Passengers were pushing forward. Evan was so close, their faces were nearly touching.

'Better any old Elven than a human, huh?' she whispered. 'Even though you don't trust him.'

'You trust his sister,' he muttered.

'I don't.'

'You hung around with her yesterday.'

She gripped his arm as the train braked and jerked. 'They shouldn't come to see this mystery woman. They might mess everything up.'

He shook her away. 'I didn't want them here, either. But Loki found out that we'd been given the name of someone who could help.'

Nell frowned. 'And you told them the address?'

'No. They insisted on coming along.' He flicked her a glance. 'It's too late. Rather them get in trouble than you.'

'That's my choice. And maybe it's not too late.'

He began to say something, but she shook her head in warning. The train slid to a halt, and Loki and Laki were weaving down the carriage towards them.

She followed the others through the station, with Laki skipping about, talking to people and cheeking the guards. She let them get ahead.

'I've got a call,' she shouted. 'I won't be a moment.'

She dialled a number.

'Dad?'

There was a sigh. 'Hello, Nell.'

'I know you're following us.'

Another sigh. 'Want a job at my place, as a detective? We could use your skills.'

'Nan's told you, hasn't she?'

'Yep. And I don't want you anywhere near that Elven boy. Or his cocky-looking mate and the girl in the inappropriate clothes. You can come straight home.'

'I can't, Dad. You have to trust me. I know what I'm doing.'

There was a grunt from her dad. 'We'll see about that, when I catch up with you.' There was a blaring of horns

121

and he swore. Good, it sounded as though he was stuck in a jam. She ended the call and ran back to them.

'That was my nan,' she lied. 'So exciting.' She turned to Evan. 'More news on the mystery woman.'

He squinted at her. 'What?'

'You know Dru said Miss Dawn might know something about the harps? Well, she's actually spoken to her now. And it's true. Miss Dawn has all the information we need.' She smiled at Laki and Loki who were watching her like cats. 'She's waiting for us, now. All we have to do is walk in and she'll give us the information. Your world is saved!'

Evan just stared at her. It was Loki who reacted.

'Hey, you're the best,' he said with a very dangerous grin. 'What are we waiting for? Let's go.'

She saw him glance at Laki as they walked outside into the biting cold. There was one taxi waiting by the kerb.

'We'll take that,' said Loki, leading the way. 'My treat.' He gave Nell and Evan an innocent smile. 'What's the address?'

'Fifty-three, St Stevens Road,' said Nell before Evan could speak.

Loki gave a laugh. 'Thanks!'

In the blink of an eye he'd grabbed Laki's hand and they were inside the taxi and slamming the door. Nell heard the doors lock. Loki was leaning forward, saying something to the driver. Immediately the engine revved and the taxi jerked away at speed. Nell caught a glimpse of the driver's face; he looked half hypnotized.

Evan watched the taxi disappear out on to the main road. For the first time that morning he met her eyes. This time his weren't so cold.

'Clever.'

She nodded. 'Thank you. And now we know why Loki and Laki are here. To stop you saving the Elven world.'

He stared after the taxi. 'Why would they do that? Why would they want their own world to die. It makes no sense.'

'They have other plans. Laki told me. I don't know what they are.' She began walking. 'Follow me. We don't need a taxi. It's just round the corner. We'll be there in five minutes.'

The sky had clouded over and snowflakes as big as goose feathers had started falling.

Nell brushed the snow off the street sign. It said 'Holy Bones Lane'. This was the place.

All around there were office blocks and flyovers, but the little lane ahead of them through the archway was old. It looked like the set of a Dickens film. The snow

123

had turned to brown slush in the city streets, but here it was untouched. No one came here. Nell didn't blame them. As the wind blew bitterly through the arch behind them, it was making an eerie noise, like a choir of ghost children singing one moment, and the next, like an old man whistling.

'I don't like it.' Evan was squinting at some dots in the sky. 'The birds don't fly over, they're veering away. It's a trap.'

Nell pushed past him. 'Don't come, then.'

She hoped she sounded braver than she felt. The church squatting in front of her and blocking the end of the lane was not helping. The bricks were sooty, and the towering walls were covered in ivy. Stained glass windows peered out between the creeping leaves like eyes between hair. The steeple had scaffolding round it, and along the roof, a row of little bushes had managed to grow up, like shaggy eyebrows.

It was definitely watching her.

'There's something wrong with this place.' Evan turned to her. 'I don't want you getting in trouble. Your grandmother and your father were following you, weren't they? I saw them, too.'

'Yes, but it'll take them ages, because of the snow on the roads.' Nell stared at the church. 'I'm sure Nan wouldn't have sent us into danger.'

Evan didn't look convinced. 'She nearly let Gwen get killed.'

'That was because she was obeying rules. She had a choice this time, and she still told me about this place.'

She forced herself to walk up to the big oak door. A buckled rusty cross was hanging crookedly above it. There was a sign, faded and bleached with age.

'The Church of the Holy Bones.' She shivered. 'But whose bones?'

Evan didn't answer. He stood with his hands in his pockets, staring at the door. It was massive, with iron studs and a huge iron ring as a knocker. Nell ignored the knocker and tapped the door lightly, with her fist. Nothing happened. So Evan reached over and banged it, filling the air around them with echoes. For a moment, as they died away, Nell thought she heard murmuring on the other side of the door. Like children whispering before a teacher came into class.

Evan kicked the door and it creaked open. The murmuring stopped.

'It wasn't locked?'

He walked in. 'Why would it be, they're going to pull the place down.'

She followed before she lost her nerve, letting the great

door slam behind her. A waft of incense-laden air swept over her, like something breathing in her face. The noise disturbed a few pigeons who'd made their homes in the corners of the oak roof. They came fluttering out like phantoms.

No, stop it. Don't think about ghosts, or things breathing in your face.

She stayed with her back against the ancient oak, tucking a stray lock of hair back behind her ear. The church was like a monstrous dark cavern after the snowy brightness outside. Most of the stained glass windows were boarded up, but some were letting in beams of crimson-coloured light, and giving the air a dark red tint.

'Hello,' she called. 'Is Miss Dawn here, please?'

There was no reply. Evan scuffed his feet, his shoulders up round his ears.

'Um. Anyone home?' Suddenly she wanted to laugh. Not happy laughter. Nervous, freaked laughter. It was too quiet, too eerie. She took a deep breath and steadied herself. 'It's really important.'

Her words echoed, but nothing stirred.

She wasn't fooled, though. She could still feel someone watching them.

They walked farther inside. Most of the pews were

pushed together against one wall. It looked like dossers or kids had been in. There were bottles and cans all over the patterned floor tiles, and a scattering of cheap disposable lighters. For some reason every surface was glittering like tinsel. She ran her hand along a pew. Frost! That's why everything glittered; it was as cold in here as it was out in the street.

'Sorry. We knocked first!' Her voice echoed again, but no one answered.

By her side, Evan's foot crunched on something. He looked down. 'Bones.'

Again, she wanted to laugh. 'Please let them be KFC.'

She stepped carefully around the remains of a bonfire that had cracked the stone tiles beneath. A few snowflakes like diamond dust were drifting gently down and making a small silvery, whispery sound as they landed. She looked up. The fire had been lit beneath a hole in the high arched roof.

'Look at these.'

Evan was walking along the far wall. It had little alcoves along it and each one had a life-size marble statue seated in it. No, not every alcove had a statue. Two were empty. The first one and the last. The last one was cracked from top to bottom, as though it had been struck by a lightning bolt.

'Maybe they're saints,' she said. 'And it's their bones kept here.'

The nervous laughter bubbled up again. She put her hand over her mouth. The seated statues looked like old, old people waiting in grim little bus shelters for the number fifty to come along. Or posed dead bodies.

I wish I hadn't thought about dead bodies.

She walked quickly over to Evan, her boots crunching on the frosted tiles. Close up the statues were worse. The marble they'd been chipped from had blue veins that ran across their white cheeks. Moss had grown on some of their shoulders, and the ridges and dents that made up their faces and the folds of their clothes had been colonized by small black lichen that made them look as though they'd been outlined in pencil. Icicles hung down from their hands and hair. Nell looked along the line.

'Definitely not saints,' she said, with a shudder. 'They don't even look holy. They look fierce and proud.'

Some had crowns, some had veils, some had wreaths of leaves around their heads. Their blind eyes stared arrogantly at her and Evan. She heard him catch his breath. They were probably freaking him out, too.

'I hate staring eyes,' she said, to break the silence. 'I used to turn my teddy bear round before I went to sleep, because it stared.'

'We should leave,' muttered Evan. 'Quickly.'

Suddenly, she lost her nerve, too. 'Maybe you're right.'

'I am right.' He couldn't take his eyes off the statues. He grabbed her hand and pulled. She could feel him shaking.

It was too late. There was a movement in the shadows by the altar. A door creaked. Nell squinted into the darkness.

''Scuse. Sorry. Is Miss Dawn here, please?' she called, trying not to let her voice shake.

The door creaked open further, letting in a beam of daylight from a window beyond. A woman was silhouetted there. Startlingly tall, she was leaning against the door frame. White-haired, white-faced. She was wearing some old clothes that hung in rags, colourless with age.

Evan's hand gripped Nell's harder. 'Not safe. Really not safe. Come on.'

'Is she a bag lady?' she whispered.

'No,' he gasped.

The woman walked closer. No, she didn't walk closer, but somehow she moved nearer. Her eyes were closed.

Not gliding, don't let her be gliding.

'We've done it now,' said Evan.

The woman came right up to them and opened her eyes. They were like black jewels. Her face was like marble. Nell was paralysed with fear. Her feet were stuck to the floor. The woman held out a hand and touched her cheek. Nell nearly fainted. Her hand was like stone.

Oh Lord.

The empty alcove, the missing statue.

'Skin like marble. Eyes like black sapphire,' croaked Evan.

His words jolted against a memory. He'd said that before. When? In the Elven forest. And Nan said it when they'd been talking about the making of the world.

'The Vanir?' she whispered.

The woman tilted her head to one side. Her marble lips seemed to be trying to open. Evan swallowed and nodded.

'It's Aurora,' said Evan.

Eight

Nell clutched her ears, desperately.

'Please. We just wanted to ask you something.'

The marble woman was hissing, angrily, like a kettle getting ready to explode.

Evan was staring like a snake. 'Don't move, don't move,' he chanted, as though it was an option and Nell's feet weren't rooted to the spot.

Miss Dawn. Of course. The goddess of dawn was called Aurora.

A blue vein on the woman's forehead began to stand out more. Then for the first time her mouth moved. There was a cracking sound and a grating creak as though her jaws were moving after a long time. Her lips parted.

The hissing turned into words. 'Ffffire, fffffflame, warmthhhhhhhhh.'

At last Nell came unstuck. She clutched Evan's hand.

'We run. Yes?'

'Too late. Stay still. No sudden moves.'

Nell felt a movement behind her, a swirling of the icy air. Something heavy crunched down on to the tiles. The ground shook. Then another mini-earthquake bang. And another, and another. One after another like . . . like . . .

Please don't let it be what I think it is.

'Oh no, oh no, oh no,' said Evan.

A chorus of creaking and grinding started up, stone screeching against stone. It was worse than fingernails down a chalkboard. Nell couldn't stand it any longer. She swung round.

The statues weren't in their alcoves any more. They were creaking to their feet, shaking off icicles like raindrops. Some were already taking steps towards her, with a sound like metal chairs being dragged across stone tiles. Frost cascaded from them. They were turning from marble to flesh, but there wasn't much difference, they were still white and veined with blue. Pairs of gemstone eyes blinked away dust. How long had they been sitting there?

'All the Vanir,' whispered Evan. She could feel his hand trembling. 'All our gods. Here?'

He was right, it was too late to run. They were pinned now, in the centre of them. Aurora was making chewing movements with her mouth, as though getting her jaw working again. She blinked her black sapphire eyes and pinned them on Nell.

'Ffffire, fffffflame, warmthhhhh,' she hissed again. She stopped, wriggled her jaw and tried again. For the first time her mouth opened properly.

'Fire,' she managed, in a low, rusty, creaking voice. 'Did you bring some?'

Nell stared back, bewildered. 'No. But we can make a fire.'

The others were crowding closer, stamping their marble feet and rubbing their petrified hands. One, who was taller than the others, pushed forward and stomped over to Aurora and stood next to her. His face was dominated by a sharp, hooked nose, with the rest of his face and hair slicked back as though he'd been formed in a wind tunnel.

'Arn!' groaned Evan. 'The Eagle.'

Arn poked his head forward and glared at Nell. She managed not to move. He did look as fierce as an eagle, as though he might peck her head off at any second.

'Make us fire,' he growled.

Evan let go of her hand. 'I'll get some wood. You look around for any full bottles of booze.'

Nell backed away and began kicking through the

rubbish. Out of the corner of her eye she could see them watching, as they stamped and creaked and came back to life. Her foot clinked against something. A bottle half full of a clear liquid. The label was torn off but when she took the top off it made her eyes water, so it was strong. She took it back and handed it to Evan. He stood back from a pile of splintered wood and cardboard he'd constructed and sprinkled it with the alcohol. He flicked one of the lighters. There was a *whump*. As the flames licked higher, he threw a few more pieces of broken pew on to his makeshift fire.

With a chorus of sighs, like gates creaking in the wind, the Vanir drew round it and held out their stony hands, the flames reflecting on their white marble faces.

Arn the eagle-man held his creaking arms out to the flames.

'S'good,' he grated. 'Fire keeps us from becoming fossils. Keeps a flicker of life in us.'

Aurora gave a huge, drawn-out 'Ahhhhhhhhhhhh'. Then she put her hands together and cracked her knuckles with a noise like ball-bearings clashing together. She twisted her head from side to side, and shrugged her shoulders a few times.

'That's better,' she rasped.

Nell felt an ice-cold hand close round her arm. Aurora

dragged her forward into the circle. Arn was doing the same to Evan. The heat of the flames beat on her face.

As the Vanir crouched down and watched, Aurora peered at her. 'And now, as we thaw, we find out who has disturbed us,' she rasped.

Arn was looking from Nell to Evan, a look of stony distaste on his marble face. 'Elven and human? Can't be good.'

Evan tried to get his arm free. 'We thought you died,' he said. His fear was fading and being replaced by a disappointed anger. 'But you're living here? In a dump like this?'

'We didn't die,' growled Arn. 'We got weak after making the Elven world.'

Aurora's grip tightened on Nell's arm, as though she was getting upset. 'We got sick,' she hissed.

One of the other Vanir looked up wearily from the fire. 'You kept asking us for things. We wanted to sleep.'

Aurora nodded. She let Nell go and dropped her arm as though moving had already tired her. 'It's true. We came here for a bit of peace.'

Evan managed to wrench himself free from Arn. 'You're our gods! You made our world. You shouldn't be *here*.'

'Even gods get old.' Aurora sighed. 'We've outlived our uses. You don't believe in us any more.'

One look at Evan's face and Nell could see that was true. He knew hardly anything about them. He was scared, but he didn't look as though he wanted to worship them. And Aurora didn't look like a god as she pulled up an old crate and sat on it. Even ferocious Arn gave a sigh and crouched down, squatting on his toes by the fire, like a bird perched on a branch.

The fire was burning fiercely now, and a wave of heat enveloped the front half of Nell. On either side the stony Vanir radiated out cold. A silence fell. She tried to think of something to say or do. But how did you persuade a god to help you? Evan was staring round as if he'd like to kick them into life.

Eventually Aurora looked up. 'How did you find us?'

A circle of eyes turned to her.

'Druscilla Church sent us.'

Arn's eyes narrowed. 'A human knows we're here?'

But Aurora recognized the name. 'Ah yes. The Watcher. She was true to me, once.'

And Nell thought she saw a slight thawing in Aurora's gemstone eyes.

'Druscilla did me a favour a long time ago. If she sent them, then there would be genuine need.'

'There is.' Evan stepped forward, his face as stony as theirs. 'The harps are stopping. The Elven world *you* made is dying.'

There was a chorus of sighs. Someone murmured, 'As we thought. It was never going to last for ever.'

'And it's not our problem any more,' snapped Arn.

Evan gave a cry of rage. 'But you're the Vanir. We thought of you as gods.'

'Gods!' scoffed Arn. 'We were the ones who lived the longest, we just carried on and on. After a thousand years we became something else instead of flesh and blood. We reached another stage. Now I don't think we'll ever die, we'll just turn to stone.'

Nell pointed to the last alcove, the one with the crack running across it.

'There's twelve of you. The last alcove is empty. One of you died.'

A silence fell. No one looked at anyone else. Aurora stared at the empty alcove for a moment, then flipped her hand.

'One of us left, that's all. There was a fight.'

Nell looked round at the circle of faces. It was like looking at a load of grumpy old people who'd had a falling-out. But they weren't grumpy old people. They were beings who could make a world.

And let it die, if they felt in enough of a mood.

She turned to Aurora. The warmth from the flames

seemed to have melted the stoniness from the woman's face. She looked almost flesh and blood. More so than Arn, who still looked like a fierce statue of a hybrid eagle-man.

'You have to go back to the Elven world and restart the harps,' she pleaded. 'Then you can come back here and we'll never bother you again.'

A bad-tempered murmuring swept round the circle, but Aurora's face was more sad than angry. She reached up and touched Nell's cheek gently with her stone hand.

'We can't. We can hardly move. We haven't been outside the church in a hundred years. We'd never make it through the mist. And if we did we'd probably get poisoned as easily as humans.'

Nell knew what she meant. A night and a day, that's all the time a human could spend there before a return to the human world would prove fatal.

'You could try,' she insisted.

Aurora shook her head sadly, and her long hair moved and creaked like branches in the wind. 'We've been here too long. The Elven will have to learn – what will be, will be.'

There was another angry cry from Evan. 'But you're powerful! You can do anything.'

Aurora's face morphed into a peeved expression. 'Ha.

Once. But making the Elven world crippled us.'

Nell stamped her foot. 'How difficult can it be? You did it once before!'

Arn clicked his tongue angrily. It was like metal ringing against stone. 'Here's how we did it. Aurora got us all together. We stole a piece of your world, twisted it out of your time and space, hid it through the mist. Now go.'

'Yes. But how did you make the harps start singing?'

'Ask your mamas and fathers,' said Aurora.

'They can't remember,' said Evan. 'They don't know how. Anyway they're imprisoned. We've freaked the human world out. They hate us.'

'You're telling me.' Arn laughed, nastily. 'That's why we made another world all those centuries ago.' He turned and snarled at Nell. 'To get away from you. Now leave us alone. Let us rest in peace.'

'No.' Evan glared at him. 'Tell me how to do it, and I'll go.'

A ripple of sour laughter ran round the circle. Nell went and joined Evan.

'Don't you dare laugh at him,' she said, turning on her heel to look at each one of them. 'He's right. If you can't be bothered, then at least tell us how to start the harps.'

There was no laughter this time, just silence. The

Vanir looked shiftily at each other and began to mutter. It was like hearing a bitter wind blowing through a deserted building.

'They've forgotten,' whispered Nell in horror.

Aurora stood up. 'Be quiet,' she grated, and everyone fell silent. Even Arn. She turned to Nell. 'We might have forgotten, but it is written down.'

She pointed to the row of alcoves. Nell saw that the stone wall between the first and second alcove had an inscription carved into it. She ran over, pulled her sleeve over her hand and brushed the frost away. A jumble of lines and triangles and little arrows appeared.

'I can't read it.'

Evan was beside her. 'It's runes.' He rubbed his sleeve across it again and began to read out loud.

> *'And so it was that Elven and human,*
> *In deep midwinter, by frosty moonlight,*
> *Went hand in hand over the killer ice,*
> *To play the new world into being.'*

Nell stared at him. 'And so it was that Elven and *human*?'

She whirled round. Aurora was behind her, reading the words herself. 'You started the harps with a human?'

Aurora narrowed her eyes as though she was looking far, far back in time. 'Yes. The Elven and humans acknowledged each other in those days.'

'Who was he?'

'A friend.' She smiled as though remembering something exciting. 'It needed both human and Elven to set the harps singing. Two sets of vibrations. That way the Elven world remained tethered to the human one. We didn't drift away.'

Nell turned to Evan. 'Me and you. We have to do it.'

Before Evan could say anything, Arn was there.

'She'll die,' he said, giving Nell a haughty look. 'She won't make it across the winter lake.'

Nell glared back. 'I might. At least I'll try – instead of sitting round here like statues!'

His face changed in an instant. It morphed. His nose became a great hooked beak that shone like bronze, his hair curved back into golden feathers. His hands reached out to grab her, the fingers with long nails like talons. Nell cringed back but hit the wall behind.

As his claws closed in on her shoulder, something hit him round his feathered head and knocked him sideways.

'Arn. Stop,' snapped Aurora.

He growled and lashed out with his lethal beak, but

the eagle feathers faded, and his face began morphing back into his usual bitter, angry features.

Nell turned her back on him, and found Evan frowning at her, but talking to Aurora.

'He's right. Nell shouldn't come. It's too dangerous. I'll get someone else. Anyone.'

Aurora shook her head. 'No. It has to be someone who is in tune with you. Someone whose soul is twinned with yours. Only then will all three – harp, Elven and human – be in tune.' She took Nell's hand, and then grasped Evan's in her other hand. 'You two are in tune. That's the tragedy for her.'

Nell could feel her hand freezing as Aurora held it.

'See?' she said to Evan. 'It's me and you, or nothing. I'm going and that's that.'

But her teeth had begun to chatter. She was still Nell the worrier, even though she'd bravely entered the forest to get Gwen. She could never forget racing against the clock, trying to get back from the Elven world before she and Gwen aged a hundred years in a few moments. So why was she doing this?

Because I have to do it. I can't not. That's all she could come up with.

'Everything counts,' she said to them both, but mainly to Evan. 'Every action sends ripples spreading out.

I followed Evan into the woods, and things happened from there.'

She was caught in the ripples. She had to see it through to the end.

Aurora squeezed her hand. 'And my human didn't die,' she said.

Arn wasn't convinced, though. He fixed her with fierce eyes. 'Why does a human girl help an Elven?'

'Because I don't want to see their world destroyed.'

'Because you don't want to share your world,' he sneered.

'I wouldn't mind. I'd love it,' she said, as he began striding up and down, his joints creaking. 'But it would frighten a lot of people if they suddenly discovered the Elven. There would be fights and battles. I hate fighting. If the Elven world is healed then it can go back to how it was when my nan first became a Watcher. Easier.'

Evan looked at Aurora. 'What do we have to do?'

'You need to go to the Mother Harp in the centre of the winter lake.' Aurora's marble face went even blanker for a moment. She's forgotten, thought Nell, in panic. Then Aurora started talking again.

'There are words. I've forgotten them for now. But they are carved on the harp.' She looked at Evan. 'Runes. You must both say them. Their vibrations should start the

Mother Harp.' She gave a harsh, stony laugh. 'But you'd better pray that it works.'

'Tell her what she'll face on the way,' said Arn. 'It's not only the harp that will try to kill her.'

Nell's heart sank, but she said, 'Stop it, you're just trying to frighten me. I'm tougher than I look.'

'Tell her,' said Arn.

Aurora pointed to the broken alcove.

'The one who sat there was called Krake. There was a fight, he went back to the Elven world. To the winter lake. Some Elven followed him. They became the Ice Elven. They and Krake want nothing to do with anyone but themselves.'

Krake. Laki had mentioned him. So that's whom she hated. A renegade Vanir.

'You will have to go past him to get to the Mother Harp,' said Arn. 'He will know you are there.'

Aurora sighed. 'If Krake doesn't want the harps restarted, the Ice Elven will not let you pass.'

'We've still got to try,' said Evan. 'It's our only chance.'

Aurora put her hands on Evan's shoulders and her black sapphire eyes stared straight into him.

'I see into your mind, Evan Harmony River. Your heart is true. I hope you succeed.'

He gave her a look, half full of hope, half angry.

'There's no one else. We have to try. We don't have a choice.'

Aurora turned her face away. 'Then go. Leave us alone.' She gave them both a push. It was like being tapped by a bulldozer.

They walked to the door and pulled it open, struggling against the wind that had picked up.

Once outside they looked at each other.

'Jeez. Now we run,' said Evan.

It was snowing hard. They hunched their shoulders, and holding hands they ran back down the old lane, through the arch and into the real world of offices and stores and cars and shoppers hurrying along.

Nell had to stop to catch her breath.

'Harmony?' she said, feeling laughter bubbling up again. This time with relief. 'Your name is Evan *Harmony* River?'

His infectious grin appeared, the first time she'd seen it since he came back from Kamchatka.

'Don't,' he said. 'You're finding out all my sad secrets.'

They began running again, skidding on the new snow covering the older ice. As they crossed a road, Evan suddenly pulled her into a shop doorway, so they were hidden from the road.

'What?' she said.

He was looking over her shoulder. 'Just in time,' he murmured.

She glanced back at the archway cowering between the tower blocks.

A car was turning through it. It was her dad's.

Nine

It was nearly dark by the time Nell found herself hurrying down Woodbridge Road with Evan. She could see her house with the lights shining warm and welcoming in the quickly gathering dusk. But she didn't make it back there.

Waiting by the alley that led to the woods were all the Elven. Falcon had lined them up along the church wall, where Gwen and her friends sat in summer. Now there were haloes of frost round the streetlamps and some low-level mist creeping around the gravestones behind the row of white-haired children.

This was all that was left of the Rivers great-family. She smiled at Falcon's little brother, Bean, as he sat on Lily's knee and played with the end of her long white hair. Next were the two insanely cute little girls, Pixie and Fay, waving and smiling as they perched on the knees of Sky and Crystal. Sitting beside them was Storm, drumming his heels on the wall. And at the end, arms folded, and determined not to smile back at her, were Rex and Bran, looking ready for battle.

Star was missing, but then there was a movement in the dark alley and she appeared, the mist swirling around her, as she led a tall thin boy, with a shock of white Elven hair. Nell caught her breath. It was Fen! Even though he looked ill and wrecked, like someone who'd been drinking all night, he still looked like a bad-boy celebrity.

You're not, though. Nell watched him come closer. You're frightening and mad and powerful.

You kidnapped Gwen.

You hexed her.

You bullied me.

You hit Evan.

You nearly imprisoned us in a dying land.

I hate you.

Evan had been greeting the little Elven and giving them hugs, but now he rushed back to her side.

'Stay cool,' he said quietly. 'You don't know. Things are different now.'

Nell shrugged him away. 'So? Doesn't mean I have to forgive him.'

Star was leading Fen by the hand. As they went by, he

didn't look at her, but gazed around as if he couldn't remember ever coming to this world and causing chaos. Star led him to the wall and he sat down, and wrapped his arms round himself in a bear hug and rocked.

I've seen that before, Nell thought. When her aunt had had her nervous breakdown, she rocked, she stared at nothing. He didn't look like a time bomb waiting to go off any more, but he still scared her.

Star and Falcon came over.

'The harp screech is getting shorter. And the earthquakes worse,' Star explained. 'Faolan and the other wolves ran off into the forest.'

'They've been howling non-stop,' said Falcon. 'They know something bad's going to happen. We had to get everyone out. The little ones were screaming and crying. They thought the ground was going to break up beneath them.'

Maybe it would, if they didn't do something soon.

'We've found a way to start the harps,' said Evan.

Star clasped her hands together and beamed at them. 'I knew you would!'

'We have to go over the winter lake and reach the Mother Harp.'

Star's smile faded. But Falcon immediately said, 'I'll come with you.'

Evan shook his head. 'Sorry, Fal. It has to be me and Nell. Elven and Human.'

A sulk settled on Falcon's face.

'You have to guard everyone,' Evan told him. 'You have to stop Loki and Laki following us.'

'When do you go?' Star looked at Evan, and then at Nell.

Nell took a deep breath. 'Tonight. The sooner the better.' Get it over and done with, she didn't add. Before I change my mind.

She looked up. A few snowflakes were drifting down on them.

'But first, we get everyone inside.'

The pavilion warmed up quickly when Falcon and Evan got the stove going. Nell went round and made sure that there were no gaps in the boards covering the windows so that no light leaked out. Then she lit a couple of the lanterns left from the party.

Soon the smallest ones were wrapped in quilts and curled up on the sofas and armchairs. Star was handing out bowls of cereal, and everyone was relaxing when the door crashed open.

Gwen sprang into the room and then came to a confused halt. She looked around, her mouth falling open.

'What? Who the hell are you lot?'

The Elven stared back, too surprised by this intrusion to say or do anything. Nell groaned. She ran up to her sister.

'What're you doing here?'

'I left my iPod here, and I . . . I . . .' Her voice tailed off as she stared over Nell's shoulder.

Nell knew who she was staring at, even before she turned round.

Fen was sitting in an armchair, still bear-hugging himself, and still rocking quietly. Gwen looked like someone mesmerized, her eyes beginning to go diamond bright. A couple of tears formed on her eyelid.

'Who's he?' Her voice quivered.

'Um. Just someone.' Nell looked around desperately. 'Evan! Quickly. Here. Do your charm. Quick.'

Gwen pointed a finger. It was shaking. 'Seriously. Who is he? I know him.'

'No. Yes.'

But it was all right now. Evan was at her side. Bees were buzzing. Falcon was coming up on the other side of Gwen. She was being charmed from both sides. Gwen wasn't immune, so why were two tears sliding down her face, and more hanging on her eyelid? Why was she still looking at Fen, and remembering him?

Why was she now stalking over to him, with her famous angry Gwen stomp that made most boys run for cover.

She went right up to him. 'Hey.'

He looked up and winced as though someone had stuck a dagger through his head.

'Do I know you?' she demanded. He didn't say anything. 'Yes. Yes, I do. I do know you.'

Fen closed his eyes and leaned back, as though he didn't want to see her. Gwen spun round and stormed back over to them. Evan and Falcon watched her in horrified amazement, and upped the charm. Gwen batted the air around her as though swatting an annoying bee.

'Nell, I don't want him around here.' Her face crumpled. 'Tell him to go away.'

'I'll get Falcon to take him somewhere else,' said Evan, quickly.

Nell caught his arm. 'No. Wait.'

She remembered all those drawings Gwen had been doing. And hearing her pacing her room and muttering to herself at night, and all that restless worrying that was so unlike her sister.

Somehow, deep down, Gwen had remembered Fen. Hiding him wouldn't make her get any better.

'Maybe she should see him,' she said.

Evan frowned. 'It's a gamble. I don't know what's going on in Fen's head any more.'

'I think he's had a breakdown,' said Nell. 'My aunt had one. You get over it in time.'

They didn't get the chance to find out, because the door slammed open again, and there was Loki. He strode in on a blast of wind and snow, with Becca dragging along behind him.

He didn't look cute any more. He looked deadly. His ice-cold silver eyes roamed round the room until he found Nell.

One moment he was at the door, the next he was in her face.

'You tricked me. I hate that.'

A split second later, Evan was there beside her. He pushed Loki away. 'Leave her.'

Loki's face went stony. He pushed back and they bounced apart, like two magnets with the same poles together.

'Stop it. Don't fight,' she said.

Loki blinked and then tried to get his rascally smile back on his face. 'You wait. You'll be sorry,' he said lightly.

Gwen went and got hold of Becca and dragged the girl over to Fen, who now had his eyes closed.

'Do we know this person? Did he do something wrong?'

Becca just stood there and said nothing. It was as though she'd stopped thinking for herself. Loki, without taking his eyes off Nell, clicked his fingers and said something rapidly to Becca. Maybe it was some sort of key word, because Becca seemed to come alive.

'Yes, he did do something wrong,' she said. 'He's Nell's friend. He hurt you, Gwen, and it's all Nell's fault.'

Nell pushed past Loki and grabbed Becca's arm. 'Shut up. You don't know anything.'

But now Gwen was frowning at her, and her eyes had gone very shiny again. 'Is it true, Nell? This *person* here hurt me and you *knew*?'

'She's talking rubbish,' said Nell, quickly. 'Loki is making her crazy.'

Becca pulled her arm away. 'As if. You're the one who's crazy!'

And now Fen was waking up again, and he and Gwen were staring at each other.

'She's been keeping lots of secrets from you,' Becca said, spitefully. 'Ask her what really happened in the woods, when you got lost.'

Nell wanted to smack her. 'Becca. Shut up.'

Becca poked a finger at her. 'No, Nell, I won't. I'm sick of you.'

'I never did anything to you.'

Becca screwed her face up. 'Your attitude! Like you know everything.' Her eyes went sly. 'Well, I know stuff now.'

Gwen tore her gaze from Fen. 'What? What do you know, Becca?'

'These are her secret friends.' Becca swept her other hand round to indicate Evan and Falcon and all the others, who were standing silently round and watching. 'They're dangerous. They're the ones who nearly killed you in the woods.' She linked her arm through Gwen's. 'Come on, let's go get a coffee with Loki. Let's leave Nell with her freaks.'

There was a whirl and Loki was standing next to them. His eyes were sparkling. He touched Gwen on the shoulder and peered into her eyes 'You believe Becca, don't you?'

Whatever he'd done to Gwen, it worked immediately, unlike the Elven charm. Gwen blinked and nodded.

'What fun we're going to have,' he said.

'No.' Nell didn't want her sister anywhere near Loki. She stood in front of Gwen. 'Please. Don't go with them.'

But Gwen had got her super-bitchy ice-queen face on. ''Scuse me, little sister. But why've you been lying to me?'

'It's not like that.'

Gwen looked unconvinced. 'I really thought you'd saved me,' she said, coldly. 'But you got me into trouble in the first place.'

Nell turned on Loki. She poked him in the chest.

'Leave Gwen out of this; I mean it. Stop trancing her.'

He laughed. 'I'm scared.'

Nell looked at Becca, who was standing as if half in a dream. Becca, who like Gwen was usually so sharp about people, had been totally taken over by a boy a couple of years younger than her. Who, if he'd been normal, they would have petted and made a fuss of for a while and then dumped when they got bored of him, because really they liked older boys not younger.

For a moment she felt sorry for Becca for being taken in by Loki.

'And leave Becca alone, as well,' she said.

That surprised Loki. Or at least he pretended to be surprised. He didn't seem to have a genuine emotion in his body. 'Why worry about Becca? She really doesn't like you.'

'So? Leave them both alone.'

'No. You'll have to come and find me.' He turned to go, but Nell moved and got in front of him.

'What's your problem?'

He wrinkled his nose and tried to go cute again, but

she could see he was boiling with anger and spite. 'You ran away. You're keeping secrets from me.'

'Because we don't trust you. You're not just here to get back your gold. Your world is dying but you don't care. Instead you try to stop me and Evan saving it.'

He didn't say anything. He frowned instead, and then concentrated on her face, his eyes focusing in on her.

'Nell, get back,' she heard Evan say.

But it was too late. Something terrible was happening to her. Something she remembered from last year, but which she thought she'd cured. Goose bumps were only the start. Then she felt a shower of fear and ice down her spine. And then it was as though someone had poured a bucket of pure dread over her. She began to breathe too fast, so fast she couldn't get a proper breath, because her chest had gone tight.

She was having a panic attack.

She'd been plagued by them a little while ago and her mum had taken her to see someone. He'd taught her to count her breaths. She tried this time but really she couldn't slow it down. She saw Loki lick his lips. She was going to faint here in front of everyone, or die. Maybe her heart wouldn't stand beating so fast. In fact she could feel her heart stopping. She wanted to sit down, cover her head with her arms and never move.

Then Evan was beside her and taking hold of her hand. 'Fight it. He's doing this to you.'

'Can't,' she gasped. 'Can't breathe.'

'You went through the Elven forest, Nell,' he whispered. 'Don't you know how brave that was? Don't let him do this to you.'

Another glance at Loki and she saw him grinning now. She couldn't let him win. So she fought it and fought it. She slowed her breathing, but he kept wrinkling his nose and frowning and then she'd be struggling for breath again. He wasn't going to let her win. Until suddenly the clamp on her chest eased, at the same time as Loki fell sideways. It was as though a wind had blown him. It hadn't. It was Evan's fist.

'Leave her alone.'

Loki staggered and then got his balance. He put a hand to his chin. 'Ow. You're going to pay for that, Elven.'

He raised his hand, but now the door was flying open again and Laki was there, in a flurry of black feathery hair.

'No fighting, boys,' she said, putting a hand on their chests and pushing them apart. Evan pushed her away and moved back, scowling at them both. 'And leave Nell alone.'

Loki looked at his sister in amazement.

'Why stick up for the human?' he demanded.

158

Laki folded her arms and stared him down. 'She's my little human friend.'

'Joke.'

'No. She's clever. She beat us.' Then she turned and pulled an embarrassed face at Nell. 'Sorry about my brother. He's so childish.'

Nell took a few more deep breaths and felt the panic begin to ebb away. 'What was that he did to me?'

'Fear hex. Nasty.'

Nell nodded. Even in her worst panic attack before, she'd never felt so sure she was going to die. 'Why *did* you stick up for me?' she asked.

Laki looked blank, then shrugged. 'Pfft. Who knows? I do stuff.' She glanced over her shoulder. 'It didn't work, though. My brother is still running off with your sister and her friend.'

A gust of wind blew in as the door swung open again. Loki was framed against the night sky. He looked back at Nell. Then he clicked his fingers and Becca and Gwen walked out.

Nell ran over. 'Stop it. Leave them out of this.'

He faced her. 'No. They belong to me now. And this night will be chaos,' he threatened. 'Start the harps. Or save Gwen. Your choice.'

He walked out. She started to run out after him.

She had to try and stop Gwen. She could tell her that tea was ready, or that Mum had phoned. Or Dad wanted to see her.

Evan held her back. 'It won't work,' he said, as though he'd read her thoughts. 'Loki's got control. She's tranced. Don't you see? He's trying to stop us again. But we can't let him. We have to go and start the harps.'

Nell pulled away from him. 'No. I have to see Gwen's OK first.' She ran to the door and turned back, desperately. 'A few hours, that's all. Please. Help me get Gwen back.'

Ten

Jackie was on the sofa with her feet up, when Nell rushed in.

All she'd wanted to do was check for Gwen, but the warmth of her house closed round her. She wanted to stay cocooned in there for ever. And not think of cold worlds, even colder than this one. Nor Ice Elven boys who were out to get her, nor Ice Elven girls who said they were her friend, but who were probably going to turn out to be like a venomous snake and betray her.

And she definitely didn't want to think about a race against time that might prove fatal or trap her in the collapsing Elven world.

Jackie grabbed the remote and muted the TV. 'There you are! About time you got back. Where've you been?'

Nell fiddled with her scarf, not looking at her. 'You know. Around.'

Talking to a gang of gods, the usual.

Jackie put the sound back on and patted the sofa beside her. 'Shall we watch something on catch-up? And snuggle?'

The scarf got some more attention. 'Um. Maybe.'

Which meant – not likely. Even if Gwen shows up and I know she's safe, then I've got to go and save a world.

'Have you seen Gwen?'

'Yep. You just missed her,' said Jackie. 'She came in like a whirlwind. Grabbed some sausages and marshmallows and then she was off again. You know Gwen.'

'What? Where was she going?' said Nell, trying to sound casual.

'Sledging by moonlight, apparently. Everyone's going. They're going to build a fire and roast stuff.'

So that was Loki's game. Get everyone out, away from the safety of their houses, into the cold – Ice Elven territory.

Jackie lolloped an arm over the back of the sofa and smiled at her. 'So, it's just me and you, then, Nell.'

'Um. I'm going, too.'

'You're both crazy! It's freezing out there.'

But she was already running for the stairs. She grabbed her old pine-scented fur coat from her bedroom and ran back down.

'Did Gwen say where they were meeting?'

'Not near the woods, that's all I know. I checked.'

Any mention of the woods made Jackie paranoid. Nell sometimes came downstairs in the morning and caught her staring out at the wood at the bottom of their garden, with her police face on. As though she'd like to go and arrest the trees for daring to hide her daughters for a day and a night.

If Gwen had made a point of saying it wasn't near the woods, then it probably was.

'I'm off. See you later.'

Jackie gave a sigh and aimed the remote. Nell felt a pang of guilt and sadness. She reached over the back of the sofa and planted a kiss on her mum's cheek. 'Soon, we'll sit together and watch TV.'

'I'll believe that when it happens.'

She gave her mum a big smile. 'Honest.'

Just got to survive a journey into a crumbling world first.

Hunter's Hill shone brightly in the moonlight. It was the perfect sledging course – a smooth steep slope from the woods at the top, until it flattened out and became the back gardens of houses. The snow had already been turned into lethal ice by sledgers during the day. Now it was like a white sheet of glass.

Someone had pushed an oil-drum to the top of the slope, and they were using it as a brazier. Boys were filling it with wood so that the flames leaped high and a fiery trail of burning embers and sparks spiralled up into the night sky. Anything barbecued on that was going to end up as charcoal.

Everyone was there from their estate, plus a few others. Sledges were zooming down the slope, or toppling over and crashing. One group was pushing a front door down the slope and leaping on when it got up speed.

Nell pushed through the crowd, desperately trying to find Gwen. Evan and Falcon were searching, too. She could see Loki, and Gwen wasn't with him. He'd found himself a flat piece of wood and was using it as a snowboard, and impressing everyone as he sped down the slope, curving round others and then screeching to a halt at the bottom in a shower of snow and ice.

She saw Laki watching, and hurried over.

'Can't you stop your brother?' she pleaded. 'I can't leave Gwen in his power.'

For the first time Laki wasn't laughing. She shook her head. 'No one stops Loki doing anything, don't you know that yet?'

Nell backed away. 'Why are you doing this? Why are you trying to stop us saving the Elven world?'

Laki just stared.

'Be like that, then.'

As Nell carried on her desperate search, her phone rang. She dragged it out of her pocket. It was her dad. She'd been expecting this. She took a deep breath and answered it.

'You go into that world and you'll die!' he shouted immediately.

'It's not like that!' She crossed her fingers, as she pushed her way through the sledgers. 'We only have to go to the nearest harp. We'll be back in minutes. It's not dangerous.'

He wasn't shouting now, he was roaring. 'Stop telling lies! I spoke to Aurora. She did her *I'm a marble statue, I can't speak* routine, until I found a sledgehammer and threatened to turn her into marble chippings if she didn't answer me.'

'I have to do this, Dad,' she pleaded. 'There's only me who can go. Me and Evan.'

'Why *only you*?' said Tom, sarcastically. 'Is that what he told you?'

Nell took a breath and began quoting.

'And so it was that Elven and human,
In deep midwinter, by frosty moonlight,
Went hand in hand over the killer ice,
To play the new world into—'

Tom cut her off. 'Fairytale rubbish! Magic. Destiny. I don't buy it.'

'It's not magic,' she shouted back. People were looking at her, so she lowered her voice. 'Or fairytale. It's science. The science of sound. When a glass shatters because someone sang a high note, it's not magic, is it, Dad? Same for this. Me and Evan match each other. It's going to take both of us to start the Mother Harp.'

She ended the call and switched the phone off. She'd come to the edge of the crowd and that's where she found Gwen. She was standing on her own, looking bewildered and upset.

'At last. Come on, we have to go home,' said Nell. She tugged her sleeve, but Gwen wouldn't move. Her eyes were oddly glazed. Loki's trance was working.

'Look at Becca,' she said. 'She's all over Jake. She knows we've only just split up. And she never even liked him anyway.'

Becca and Jake were walking towards them, arms

round each other, giggling about something.

'I can't believe she'd do that to me. She's out. She's not a friend any more.'

This was part of Loki's plan, Nell knew.

'So let's go home. Show her you don't care.' She pulled at Gwen's sleeve but it was like trying to move a tree.

Jake and Becca walked by. Nell waited for her sister to explode. It didn't happen. Instead Jake came back. He stood in front of them, kicking at the snow, his face confused. Behind him, Becca was standing looking lost, as though she had no idea why she was with Jake. Jake had the same look. They're all tranced, thought Nell.

'Can I have a word?' Jake said to Gwen.

Gwen flicked her hair back. 'Do you mind? I'm talking to Nell.'

He looked as though he was ready to cry. 'Please, Gwen. Talk to me.'

'What? Whilst you're with her?' She gave Becca a snake stare. Becca tossed her hair and stared back.

'I'll tell her to go away,' said Jake. Gwen tried to walk away but he got hold of her arm. 'Just talk to me.'

Nell moved between them. 'Leave her alone. She has to come home.'

For a moment Jake looked right through her, as though

he couldn't see her. Then his eyes focused on her. 'Is your name Gwen?' he snapped. 'Then shut up.'

She didn't move. 'No, I won't. Leave it for now and talk to Gwen in the morning.'

'Keep out of this, Nell,' said Gwen. She turned and shouted to Becca, 'Don't ever speak to me again, do you hear?'

Becca flounced closer. 'I hear. So what?'

Gwen and Becca, best friends since Woodbridge Primary, were going to fight. Nell knew she would never get Gwen away if she let this continue. She ran over to the rest of their gang, who'd noticed the argument and were hovering close by. 'Katy. Eve. Gwen needs you.'

They ignored her too, and continued watching Becca, Jake and Gwen, who were now shouting in each other's faces. In the end Nell had to grab Eve and shake her, before she took any notice. 'I said, go and stop the fight.'

But Eve shrugged her off. 'I'm not speaking to Gwen. She brought this on herself.' Her eyes were slightly out of focus. Nell cursed under her breath. Loki had been busy. How many more were under his spell? she wondered.

Some of the sledgers were walking over to witness the fight now. One boy came and stood next to her and shouted, 'We're on Jake's side. Go, Jake!'

Nell rounded on him. 'There isn't a side. It's an argument, that's all.'

The boy looked at her as though she was mad, but at least he saw her. 'You're kidding. It's more than that. This is important. It's about where you stand.'

'No, it isn't.'

But things just kept getting worse and worse. Arguments flared around Nell.

'It's not Gwen's fault!' someone snapped. 'Jake started it. It's him. And Becca.'

'Rubbish. Becca's right to stick up for herself. Gwen's a bitch.'

'No. Becca's being the bitch. So don't give me that attitude.'

'Fight, fight, fight,' some of the boys started chanting.

Nell felt the atmosphere change, and she couldn't do a thing about it. Loki had won. The party on the hill became something ancient and menacing and dangerous. The flames of the brazier blazed and flickered over their angry, excited faces, as though they'd returned to the Iron Age and were two tribes getting ready for war.

Nell searched the crowds for Loki and ran over to him. He was standing at the side, watching, smiling his smug smile. She really wanted to smack his face and make it go away. 'Stop it,' she demanded.

All that happened was his smile got broader.

'No wonder our leaders always insisted we keep ourselves separate.' He waved a hand at the argument now raging amongst most of Gwen's friends. 'Humans are always ready for a fight. I didn't need to do much.'

Nell walked away, heading back to Gwen, until a snowball hit her on the back of the head. More than a snowball, an ice ball. It knocked her on to her knees. It was Loki. As she turned he threw another into her face, and as she tried to wipe it away and gasp for breath, he went to hit her with another. There was a flurry of snow which twisted into a little whirlwind, and Evan was there.

'Leave me and Nell alone. Understand.'

Loki's smile wiped off in an instant. His lip curled. 'You're Forest Elven. You're nothing.' He put his hand over his heart. 'We're the real Elven. But you chose to trick me and side with a human!' He snarled at Nell. When he wasn't happy and smiling, Loki looked like a Tasmanian devil, all pointed face and sharp teeth.

Evan moved and now they were face to face, inches apart. 'Take the trances off everyone,' he ordered.

'No.' Loki snarled at him. Evan snarled back at him. Nell had seen this with the younger Elven. When girls like Pixie and Fay fought, they hissed like cats. When the boys fought, they snarled.

Nell's stomach lurched. 'Don't fight.'

What other tricks would Loki have? How much power had he got? Could he kill Evan?

Loki glanced at her. 'We will fight, Nell. Me and him. We'll fight.'

'I'm ready,' said Evan.

They both leaped at the same time, and crashed against each other. Then they were down on the snow, moving too fast to see who was winning, ice atomizing into the air around them.

'Someone stop them,' cried Nell.

No one moved, everyone gathered round as though they were hypnotized. Then she saw something, a flash of moonlight on something long and pointed and deadly. A lethal icicle, steel hard, and clutched like a dagger in Loki's hand.

'I'll stop it, then,' she muttered, looking around desperately.

Sledges had been abandoned by those watching the fight. She grabbed the biggest and with a great heave pushed it towards Loki and Evan. It skimmed across the ice and slammed into them, knocking them both off their feet and sending Loki sliding down on it. Evan slid a few metres before bringing himself to a halt.

But it wasn't over. Loki would never stop, Nell knew.

He would keep going, keep causing chaos, so she and Evan would never get away until it was too late to save the Elven world.

There was a shout from behind them. Someone had kicked over the oil-drum and it was rolling down the slope, spewing out burning branches like a giant Catherine wheel, leaving scattered smaller fires in its wake. And as though that had released a madness in all of them, not just Evan and Loki, everyone started fighting.

It was like a computer game, like Soldier of Fortune. Nothing looked real in the moonlight and the red flickering shadows of the fires. Faces loomed out at Nell, or darted away as she ran around, trying to find Gwen.

Most of the sledging had stopped, because suddenly there were more people pouring on to the hill. A whole load had turned up from another estate. There were two mobs on the snow now. At first snowballs hurtled through the air around her. Then someone hurled a rock. One boy fielded it with a burning branch and sent it speeding back at them. Someone gave a cry as it struck home. There was a pause, and then a chorus of shouts and everyone was digging for rocks, hurling ice balls, scrambling down the slope to grab burning branches, using sledges as shields, smashing DIY sledges to get clubs. The pretend screams became real screams.

Nell tried to keep track of Loki, but she couldn't. Nor Laki. It was like a war zone.

Lights were going on in the gardens down below. A siren started up.

Evan was at her side. 'The police. We have to run.'

She looked around. 'Find Gwen.'

Girls were screaming, boys were scarpering. She listened to the screams, trying to figure out which was Gwen's. But it was too late because the police were coming from all angles, advancing through the trees behind them, as the torches started up the slope in front. They were surrounded.

Someone came up behind her. 'Boo!'

It was Loki. He sounded delighted.

She swung round at him. 'Why are you doing this? Why don't you want us to fix the harps? It makes no sense!'

He gave her a sly smile. 'We have a plan. We kept our god. Not like Evan and his kind.'

There was a flurry of snow, and Laki came to a halt in front of them.

'Stop it now, Loki. Not funny any more. They could get hurt.'

Nell grabbed her arm, as the torch beams swept up the slope. 'You better tell your brother that gods aren't always

173

to be trusted. You'd be better off trusting me and Evan to save the world.'

Laki pulled a face. 'I think that sometimes.'

Nell squeezed her arm. 'You don't hate humans,' she pleaded. 'When we went shopping you had fun. You weren't pretending. Do something.'

Laki pulled her arm away. 'I'm fascinated, that's all. I like new things.'

Nell didn't wholly believe her, but the police were close now. She could hear them shouting at everyone to stay still. She could hear Gwen screaming and sobbing that her father was a cop and they'd got to let her go.

'Is that your aim? Get us arrested?' she said to Loki, who was watching the mayhem with delight. 'Well, it's gone wrong. I can hear Gwen. They've caught her. She's safe from you. So I'm off.'

Just let him try and grab me, she thought, but he didn't. As she turned to run he muttered something in Elven. Immediately she felt her feet dig through the snow as though her weight had increased. She tried to lift a foot – she couldn't.

'Very funny. Some kind of hex?'

He nodded and laughed.

'Won't hold me long,' she said. 'I'm immune.'

'A minute or two. That's all I need,' he laughed.

She tried to turn to Laki, but her feet held firm. 'Please. Take the hex off me.'

Laki appeared in front of her, wringing her hands. For the first time she looked worried. 'No. It's for the best. Seriously, Nell.' She came closer. 'Don't come into the Elven world. Something bad will happen if you do. No one argues with Krake.' Then she stepped back and faded into the night.

As the torch beams swung closer, Evan came running. 'Nell! Quick!'

Nell grabbed his hand. 'I can't move. He hexed me – I can't move.'

Loki was running towards the nearest police. 'They're over there. They started it!' he shouted, pointing back at Nell and Evan. A torch beam swung round and trapped them in a circle of white light.

'Evan, we have to go.' It was Falcon. 'The police, they stink of iron. This is bad.'

'Run,' said Evan. 'Tell Star to stay in the pavilion, on guard.'

Then he turned to Nell. 'It'll fade in a minute or two. Then we run.'

'We haven't got a minute,' she cried.

The two policemen with the torch were coming.

If she got caught, her father would never let her go. He'd lock her away to keep her safe.

The torch beam was getting brighter.

'Stay right where you are, you two,' one of the policemen shouted. 'Or you'll only get in more trouble.'

'Use your charm,' she whispered to Evan.

'Great, they won't see me, but that won't help you.'

'Watch.'

Nell began to concentrate, then decided that wasn't the way. At school it had always happened before when she was hardly trying.

I'm not here. Forget about me, she chanted to herself as the police crunched their way towards them, the torch beam flickering. She could hear the buzzing as Evan turned his own charm on. But the same sound had begun to flow around her as well. Suddenly the torch beam wavered, followed by two confused voices.

'Where did they go?'

'Who?'

The torch beam swung round and highlighted another group.

'There they are. Stay right where you are,' said one of the policemen, and they turned away and headed off in a new direction.

Nell let out a sigh of relief. It wasn't a fluke. She could

make people forget about her.

Evan was staring at her. 'You can charm? How?'

She remembered asking her nan why they were immune to the Elven. Something genetic, she'd said. Something inherited in them. In the past Elven and human could fall in love, and they could have babies. It was there in the sagas. The hero Hogni had a human mother and an Elven father. It was a drop of Elven blood in their veins that gave them the immunity. Maybe it could give them some other Elven traits, too.

'Maybe I'm turning Elven,' she said.

He tugged at her sleeve. 'Clever. Now we run.'

Jackie had fallen asleep on the sofa. The TV had a sign saying that the channel was now off air. Nell got a blanket and covered her up. Then she turned the TV off.

If this was a film she would've stopped and looked around, and touched a few things, sadly. But that wouldn't work. That way people had time to change their minds. To look at their mums and realize that they couldn't risk never seeing their homes again. So she briskly kissed Jackie, and whispered, 'Bye, Mum. See you soon. Fingers crossed.'

Then she crept straight out into the cold again. Evan was waiting by the gate, and keeping watch.

'You're sure?' he said.

'Don't start.' She pushed by him and began to run down the road, slipping on the snow and ice. She heard him following. And neck and neck they raced to the woods and through the mist.

Eleven

They stopped only when the mist was behind them and they were staring at the great frozen Elven forest. Nell felt a wave of fear flooding over her.

Can I do this? Am I strong enough? I have to be. There's no turning back once we leave here.

A night and a day, that's all the time she had. Or maybe less. Now the Harps were stopping, who knew how much time she really had?

The towering pines were immobile, frozen and heavy with snow and icicles. The snow beneath her feet had become harder, too. It creaked and crunched, and she hardly sank into it. The wind was light but it was still like facing the blower of a deep freeze. It froze the tears in her eyes.

And the silence of the harps filled every corner of the clearing. She waited, but no grating tune played.

What if they'd stopped altogether? Were they too late? No, if their music had finally died completely then those earth tremors would start pulling the world apart. She stamped her feet. The ground was solid – for now. And a few of the Elven were here, flitting from between the trees to greet them.

Star ran up and hugged her, followed by Falcon, still looking sulky.

'Let me go with you,' he said to Evan.

'No. You have to watch over everyone.' Evan turned to Nell. 'And we have to go. You ready?'

'Ready as I'll ever be,' she said, as brightly as she could.

He held out his hand. She was getting used to this, the feel of holding hands with him. This time, though, he pulled her close and put both arms round her. For a moment they were locked together, and she felt a tiny bit of warmth. Then—

'We flit,' he said.

The forest blurred. Then became a snowstorm around them. The air left her lungs. The wind became like frozen concrete, battering and bruising her. Her face felt as though it had been slapped hard. She gritted her teeth and held on to Evan for dear life, thinking, *not much longer, not much longer*. But it went on and on, until she thought she was going to pass out, and then the snowstorm slowed and became like TV static; the battering of the wind became punches, then slaps and eventually stopped. She felt Evan stumble forward as they slowed, and they both fell to their knees. She stayed crouched down, until her surroundings stopped being a blurred snowstorm and formed into scenery.

It was scenery she'd thought she'd never see again.

They were outside Evan's palace. It took her a couple of seconds to focus on it and distinguish the palace from the tangle of giant tree roots, logs, woven branches, rocks and stones.

Eventually her eyes adjusted and there it was. A dark fairytale dwelling, half alive, half wild. It seemed to be watching them from under its icing of snow. But she had something more urgent to attend to.

''Scuse.' She scrambled to her feet, ran a few steps, turned her back and stood thinking about being sick, but this time she wasn't.

'You OK?' It was Evan. 'Going to throw up again?'

She took a few deep breaths, then turned round.

'Ha, no. I must be getting used to moving faster than the eye can follow.'

She walked towards the arched tree roots that framed the great oak front door. There beside it was the memory tree, a lilac tree bare of leaves and blossom now, but still hung with photos of all the missing Elven parents, imprisoned in the iron camps of the North.

They stopped and looked at the photo of Evan's little sister, Duck. She was unmistakable because of her dandelion-clock hair. Neither of them said anything, but Nell knew he was thinking the same thing.

If they failed, and the world died, then little Duck would never, ever live anywhere but a prison camp.

Evan kicked the front door open. It had become iced over since Star led the little ones away to the pavilion. Even when they got inside, everywhere was trimmed with icicles taller than herself.

At least this time she wasn't being stalked by crazy power-mad Fen and his wolf, Thor, she thought, as she followed Evan to the great hall. And there were no Elven girls and boys looking at her with mistrust.

'Wait here,' said Evan, and hurried away.

She walked into the big room. Frost covered every surface, including the floor. And where once it had been full of Evan's cousins and cousins-of-cousins shouting and laughing, now it echoed forlornly.

So how come the big log fire in the centre was still burning?

She walked over to it, drawn by the idea of warming her hands, and discovered that a fresh pile of logs and branches had been added to it recently, and there was a further pile of chopped logs waiting at the side.

Of course, there was one person she'd met last time that she hadn't seen again.

'Lettie?' said Nell.

The pile of quilts on the seats around the fire stirred and a white head poked up.

Nell found herself confronted by the human woman, Lettice, who'd willingly imprisoned herself in the Elven world a hundred years ago. She was one of the lost girls who went through the mist and never came back out again.

'Star found you, then,' the old lady croaked. She grinned wickedly. 'And somehow managed to get you mixed up in Elven affairs again?'

'Yes.' Nell frowned. 'Sorry, but did they leave you behind?'

Lettie gave a laugh. 'Not likely. I didn't want to go with them. What for? I couldn't go back to the old world, anyway.' She patted the quilts round herself and sighed, but not unhappily. 'If the world ends, I'll go down with the harps.'

'No,' said Nell, horrified. In the back of her mind she was thinking, this could have happened to me and Gwen. Fen could've got us trapped in this dying world.

'I'll get Evan to do something. Or we'll think of a way to save you.'

Lettie took her hand. 'Shush, pet. I've had the most amazing life, and I'm too old now, anyway.' Her eyes got a faraway look in them. 'I've explored all this land. Who else can say they've lived in and explored a world other than their own?'

'Have you seen the winter lake?' said Nell.

Lettie nodded. 'When I first came here the Ice Elven hadn't cut themselves off completely, although they were very hostile. I went with our king once to the lake.' For the first time her contented smile slipped. 'A bitter, bitter land,' she whispered.

'Worse than this?'

'This is summer in comparison.' She shivered, and a look of fear swept over her face. Her eyes widened. 'And there's something under the ice.'

'What?'

'Something dangerous, that they don't talk about.'

She was glad Evan came back at that moment, so she didn't have to hear more. His arms were full of clothes. They were the same as his. 'Elven deep-winterwear. Or else you'll freeze.'

Lettie took the jacket and rubbed it between her hands. 'Wonderful. These will keep you warm, girl. The down and feathers of the Elven snow goose. I helped make some of these. They last forever. That's why we went out there, to trade clothes like this for our gold and silver. There's nothing warmer anywhere in *any* world.'

'They'll make me able to survive the winter lake?' said Nell.

'They'll help. Get in and get out fast,' said Lettie. 'Even with the goose feathers, you'll have hours, that's all.'

Nell took off her own fur coat and put the Elven clothes on. It was like snowboarding gear, in greys and whites like Loki and Laki wore, with soft black feathers trimming the hood and cuffs.

'Same colour as the snow goose. Black, grey and white,' said Evan.

There was a pair of trousers that felt light but immediately threw out warmth, as though they'd got an electric heater hidden in the fabric. Then she pulled on the hooded jacket and rolled the sleeves back. The same wave of heat flowed down her arms and round her neck. Evan handed her a pair of boots and socks. She put them on and her feet began to warm up.

Evan grinned at her. 'Now you look Elven as well as being able to charm like one.'

She looked down at herself. 'Practical. Yet fun. Gwen would be jealous.'

He straightened her hood for her. 'Come up to the top. I'll show you where we're going.'

She followed him up the spiral stairs that led through the floors of the palace. Each floor had a balcony that looked over the massive trees, but they were shuttered now against the cold. As they toiled up the stairs the wind blew in through every crevice, and through the stairs themselves. As they rose higher it got sharper and began to whine and sing. Nell felt the stairs begin to sway, and then the whole palace seemed to shift and creak as it got buffeted from all sides.

She was glad when she made it to the top, her legs cramping and a stitch starting up in her side. She came out on the roof, the wind nearly taking her feet from under her. She followed Evan across the deck to the rickety handrail – which was all that stood between them and the vast drop to the giant trees far below them. She clutched the rail and tried to stop the vertigo making her head swim.

'Concentrate on the horizon,' Evan told her. 'Don't look down.'

She forced herself to look out across the trees as they marched on for mile after mile until they faded into the far distance. Last time she was up here, fighting for her life, the forest spread out below her had been dark-green and mysterious. Now it was cobbled white, with occasional spires of black-green where the wind had blown the snow from the tallest pine trees. The sky was a mix of purple and storm-grey that hung heavily above them like an old mattress ready to split and shower the earth with lethal feathers of snow.

But nothing was as awesome as the harps.

Nell shaded her eyes from the stinging wind with one hand and held fast to the rail with the other. She looked out at those huge impossible devices, spreading out through the forest, right to the horizon. From here they seemed like tall, sturdy telegraph poles. But that was only because they were far away. Close to she knew they were wide enough to drive a car through the base. Each one was strung with cables thicker than a man's arm, that anchored them to the ground all around. It was these cables that vibrated and sang out the tune that kept the Elven world alive.

Nell concentrated on the harp nearest to her. It was a mile away but she could still see that the trees all around it had died. Some of them were still standing, like frozen skeletons, others had fallen and rotted on the ground. There were probably piles of dead birds around them, too. And the corpses of small animals. The harsh, grating dying music of the harps might hurt her ears, but she knew that it was lethal to the littlest forest creatures.

It would be lethal to her, too, if it stopped completely.

'I understand how sound can make a wineglass break. But how can it form a whole world?' she said. 'How can a tune make a world?'

'Everything is sound,' said Evan. The icy wind had blown some colour into his white cheeks. Not red though, like her face, Nell thought. No, when Elven looked really cold, they had a tinge of blue. 'Everything vibrates. All the tiniest parts of our bodies are singing like guitar strings being plucked.'

'You mean our atoms?'

'Uh-huh.' He pulled an icicle off the edge of the handrail. 'This is just water, but its atoms are vibrating slower now it's cold, and so it turns from runny water to solid ice. But if it got hotter it would vibrate faster and it would disappear and become a cloud of steam.'

'So Aurora made the harps sing a certain sequence of notes, and a piece of the human world changed?'

He nodded. 'Changed into this bubble world, that hangs on to the side of yours, like a balloon on a string.'

She wiped her eyes, which were streaming from the cold wind. 'I've been looking on Google. *In the beginning was the word*,' she said. 'That's what the Bible says. But even before that the ancient Greeks thought the stars made music.'

Evan looked up at the bruised sky. 'They do. They sing. We hear them.'

She laughed. 'Really?'

'Uh-huh. We hear more sounds than you do.'

Suddenly, he frowned. He clapped his hands over his ears. 'Which is why this is going to hurt me more than you.'

'What?'

He didn't answer. He'd squeezed his eyes tight shut.

That's when she noticed that a pressure had been building in her own ears. She'd vaguely thought it was the height making them pop. Now she knew that it wasn't. Something was building in the air, an irresistible pressure, like going too deep underwater without popping your ears. The faraway harps began to look blurred. She felt the palace below her begin to shake. It was happening again. The harps were about to play their dying notes.

'Here we go!' shouted Evan.

The sound hit them and split the air.

It was the screech of a thousand violins, all playing the wrong note but louder than a jet engine. And now it was combined with terrible undercurrents of sound, like a giant dragging a garden fork across stone tiles.

She crouched down and covered her head as it battered her eardrums. She started counting without realizing it – counting out the seconds, hoping it would stop.

Ten seconds. Ten seconds of hellish screech, instead of the constant background melody she'd first heard from the harps. Then it stopped.

She stood up in the ringing silence. The wind had dropped. She felt as though she'd got cotton wool stuffed in her ears; everything was too quiet after the tempest. Evan was staring out at the harps, his face tinged not with blue but with green now, as though he was going to be sick.

'Ten seconds,' she said. 'The worst ten seconds of my life.'

'I know.' Evan turned to her. 'Star says it was twenty yesterday. Thirty the day before. The harps are weakening by ten seconds a day.'

It was like counting the seconds to see how far away a thunderstorm was, except this was counting down to the end of the world.

'One day left,' she said. 'And that's all I have as well, before I'm imprisoned here.'

'So we better get going.'

He pointed to the dark violet line on the horizon where the forest stopped.

'That's the start of the winter lake. Remember the storm that blew over last time?'

'Yes.' She wouldn't forget it in a hurry. The rain had hit them like a waterfall, drowning out every other noise, and nearly drowning them.

'They've stopped,' he said.

'That's good, isn't it?'

'They've stopped because it's too cold even for snow.'

She couldn't tear her eyes from that thin purple line. This palace was far away from her home. But the lake was like the other side of the world. If they got stuck there, they would never be able to flit back to the mist.

'You still good to go?' said Evan, trying to read her face.

She pulled up the hood of her feather jacket and tried to smile. 'Yes, of course I am. Let's do it.'

They flitted again, Evan's arms wrapped tight around her. She kept her eyes closed against the battering air, imagining their journey as she'd seen it from the roof of the palace – the long miles through the trees to that distant dark line. The snow goose suit kept her warm but her face turned to ice, until she turned away and hid it in the front of Evan's jacket.

And then they stopped, suddenly like before, falling forwards, Evan letting go and then both tumbling the last few steps. She took her time getting up, breathing deeply, making sure she wasn't going to be sick.

That wasn't the only reason. Out of the corner of her eye she could see the last trees of the forest. In front of her she could feel a void. A nothing that breathed the iciest, deadliest air over her.

'Nell? You OK?' Evan was breathing heavily. That had been a long flit, after he'd already carried her to the palace.

'Uh-huh.'

She got to her feet and forced herself to gaze out at the winter lake.

Twelve

The bitter wind blew tiny daggers of ice into her eyes.

The thin wintery daylight had ended with the forest behind them. In front was a dark but glowing twilight. It was unearthly. The sky had every shade from purple to violet to deep grey-blue.

But it wasn't the sky that was making Nell's heart pound faster and faster. It was the winter lake – if you could call it a lake. It looked more like a sea to Nell. It stretched out before them, endless, filling the world like a black mirror, from left to right and to the farthest horizon. The harsh wind, colder than anything Nell had ever felt in her life, blew a scent of snow and ice and nothing else.

An endless frozen lake. The thing she feared most. How deep was it? No, don't even think about its depth.

She had never felt so far away from her home. From everything she knew. From warmth. She would've given anything to be still wrapped in Evan's arms, but he was crouched down at her side, still trying to catch his breath from the flit.

Through the warmth of the goose feathers she could feel little trickles of cold invading. She pulled her hood tighter round her face, so that the feather trim brushed her cheeks and caught in her eyelashes. At least that might stop the tears in her eyes freezing. She blinked a few times and managed to focus.

On the far horizon, a crazy long way away, was a black needle stark against a patch of pale violet sky.

'That's the Mother Harp?'

Evan struggled to his feet. 'Yes.'

She squinted at it, trying to work out the perspective, but there was nothing around it, no buildings or trees, to measure it by. 'How tall is it?'

He stared at it. 'Very. Our mamas tell us stories about it. How the top pierces the sky and is covered in icicles taller than the palace. If one fell it could pierce a man straight through from head to toe.'

'Urgh. Wish you hadn't told me that.' Nell's spirits sank. The Mother Harp was so far away, and when they got there they could be killed by falling icicles. If they got there in time. They only had a day at most. She turned to him.

'If you rest for a while, could we flit to it?'

He gave a grim laugh. 'I wish, but we can't flit on ice. It would be suicide. No traction. And anyway, it's too far, and the air is too cold. Even in the goose suits, we'd freeze.' He shivered and looked around as if checking that they were truly alone. 'The good thing is the Ice Elven can't flit to us either.'

He left her and walked across the last of the snow to where the lake began.

'Sorry, Nell. We have to walk.' He took a step on to the black ice.

She followed him and balanced on the edge. She looked around at the miles of ice fading into the distance. Nothing moved, except to one side, where a few black dots whirled high up in the thunderous sky.

Evan saw her looking. 'Lammergeyers. But ice ones. Much bigger than ours. Besides the snow geese, they're the only things that can survive the cold.' He held out his hand. 'Come on.'

Nell looked down at the lake at their feet.

'Not the only thing. Lettie says there's something dangerous under the ice.'

'Well, it won't bother us. We're walking on top of the ice.'

She forced her frozen face into a smile and took his

hand. They were both wearing thick gloves, but she imagined she could feel extra warmth coming through. It gave her courage. She'd come this far, she had to do this.

'Is the ice thick?'

'Of course. It never thaws.'

She stepped on to it as though it was the thinnest glass and she was the daintiest of ballerinas.

'I've got a thing about ice. I always think I'll fall through.'

'There are weak spots,' said Evan. 'See how the ice is black? If you see any white or grey spots, Lettie says they're weak places, where the Ice Elven have made holes for fishing. Don't walk on them. Then you'll be OK.'

I'll never be OK out here, she thought.

Hand in hand they started walking, dwarfed by the immensity of the lake and the massive bowl of the sky above.

'If only it was lighter,' she said. The continual low-level twilight was making her depressed.

He shrugged. 'It never gets light here. The sun never shines.'

She skidded on a patch of ice, but managed to keep on her feet. 'I don't understand how the Ice Elven can survive. I know they're not human, and they're differently alive, like you. But everything needs some warmth and sunlight, doesn't it?'

'They're used to it. My father used to tell us stories about them. As they moved closer and closer to the winter lake, farther away from us, their skin became frozen and their hearts began to beat slower and slower.'

'How can they survive without blood pumping round their bodies?'

'Their blood is nearly ice. Somehow that ice sustains them.' He pulled her closer to him and took off his glove for a moment. 'Feel my pulse.'

She took off her own glove, wincing as the bitter cold immediately nipped at her skin. Before her fingers froze she took his skinny wrist and felt the tiny blip of his heartbeat, and then a pause that lasted for a few seconds, before the next blip.

'Your heart's slowed down!' she exclaimed.

He took her wrist and felt her pulse. 'So has yours. It's the cold. Our bodies are trying to turn us to ice.' He grinned. 'At least it hasn't frozen all the goodness out of us, like it has with Loki and Laki.'

She slipped her glove back on.

'Not Laki. She was curious about us,' she said, feeling that even now she wanted to stick up for the Ice Elven girl. 'I saw her try to stop Loki. She's more open-minded.'

'Don't trust her. Forget about her,' he said, abruptly.

But now that he'd mentioned the Ice Elven, Nell couldn't stop thinking about them. Loki had tried everything to stop them coming here. He must know that they'd escaped from the police. Surely he'd be out looking for them again? The lake was big, but if all the Ice Elven, both the Stone great-family and the Thorns, put out search parties, they'd be able to spot a human girl and an Elven boy.

'Where do they live?' she asked him.

He scanned the horizon for a moment, and then pointed. 'That's one of their palaces.'

Nell squinted hard and tried to focus. Elven eyes were much better than human ones. Even so, she thought she just might be able to see a series of spires on the edge of her vision, way over to their left.

'Is that where Loki and Laki come from?'

He shrugged. 'Could be Stone or Thorn,' he said briefly, as though he'd rather save his breath for walking. But Nell needed to talk, needed to break the silence.

'Is it?' she insisted.

'Not sure. There's one for each of the two Ice Elven great-families.'

'And a Vanir to watch over them?'

He gave an impatient sigh. 'Somewhere. Yes.'

Now he'd pointed out the palace, she couldn't stop watching it. 'They might spot us.'

'It's a long way away. The ice is big.' He squeezed her hand, not to comfort her she suspected, but to make her walk faster. The more time that passed, the tenser he was becoming. 'We have to hope they don't,' he said, edgily.

They carried on walking, without talking now. After a while she relaxed a little, looking down at the ice instead of continually watching the black needle in the distance. A movement caught her eye.

She stopped. Far below the dark surface, she caught a glimpse of something slithering beneath them, something sinuous like an eel, but much, much bigger. It was gone in a split second.

'Something moved,' she said.

Evan crouched and peered at the black ice. 'The water rippling underneath, that's all.' He stood up and tugged at her hand. 'Forget it.'

Easier said than done, she thought, as they started walking again, but it seemed both their moods had taken a turn for the worse. Evan plodded grimly along, whilst Nell's spirits dipped lower and lower.

The lake was endless. Their time was short. This was useless!

Every now and then she would slip and Evan would haul her up again, and she'd feel stupid and clumsy. Sometimes the ice stopped being mirror-smooth and looked like it had frozen into the shape of ripples and waves that tripped them and made the going even slower. Then they would swear or curse, and although they kept holding hands it was more so they could drag each other to their feet, or irritably pull each other along if one got too slow. The low-level twilight wasn't helping, either.

After a long time that might have been an hour, but could have been longer, Nell clutched at her side, and tugged Evan's hand to make him slow down a bit.

'What?' he said, moodily.

'Stitch. Slow down for a bit.'

If he tuts or makes any comment, I'll hit him, she thought.

But he didn't. He began looking round nervously and then he let go of her hand and clutched his ears.

'No, no, no,' he muttered. 'Here it comes again.'

Nell pulled her hood tight and they both crouched down as the pressure grew and their ears popped. The ice began to tremble beneath their feet, and Nell fell to her knees, panic washing over her.

Please don't let the ice break up! Please don't let me fall through!

Then the screech of the dying harps rippled over them, setting their teeth on edge and drilling through their brains.

Nell cowered, and counted. '. . . six, seven, eight . . .'

The screech stopped abruptly. Nell stood up. The ice remained unbroken.

'Eight seconds. It's lost two already!' she cried.

Evan looked stricken. 'They're dying too fast. That means we haven't even got a day.'

He grabbed her hand roughly. 'Come on.'

But she planted her feet, and wouldn't walk. 'This isn't going to work, is it?' she said angrily. 'You can tell me to hurry up all you want. But we're never going to make it all the way to the Mother Harp!'

He squinted at her through his feathered hood. 'Don't say that.'

'See? I'm right.'

He let go of her hand. No, he threw it away from him. 'So what do we do, huh? Stop? Sit here? Wander back?' He pointed a finger at her. 'You're so clever, you tell me.'

He might be angry, but so was she. The thought of the ice shattering!

'We've got to move faster.'

'What? Shall we fly?' he shouted.

He stomped off again. It would serve him right if she

didn't follow. But what choice did she have? If she lost him, she would be stranded out here. She'd never be able to flit back through the forest to the mist. So she began walking again, but she kept her distance from him. She imagined what they must look like from the lammergeyers' point of view – two tiny dots on the black ice, sulkily walking apart from each other.

After a while Evan turned round and began walking backwards. All she could see was his feathered hood and the cloud of his breath. He seemed to be scanning the area.

'What's up?' she said, coldly.

'I think someone's following us.'

She looked around. 'There's no one. And there's nothing to hide behind.'

'Doesn't mean someone isn't following us. Maybe they can cloak themselves.'

She had a feeling he was playing with her, telling her scary things to make her walk faster. Just in case she was wrong, she picked up her speed and moved closer to him. 'Is that even possible?'

He shrugged, as though he didn't care whether she believed him or not. 'It was possible for us to learn how to alter your electricity. Maybe we could learn to cloak ourselves, too. Maybe the Ice Elven already know.'

'Loki and Laki can't,' she pointed out. 'Or they would've done.' But just the thought of Loki being able to become invisible made her shudder.

'So I'm imagining it,' he snapped, and walked on ahead again.

She followed him this time, and caught up.

'I wish I hadn't bothered trying to save your world. It's stupid.'

He whirled round. 'Go back to your home, then.' He stormed off.

Nell watched him go, blinking back tears. Stupid tears of frustration and anger that she'd walked into this, without ever thinking it through. She looked at the distant black needle. It hadn't grown at all. Even if by some miracle they made it to the Mother Harp, their vibrations weren't exactly in tune any more. They'd probably fail to get it started because they were angry with one another.

Evan was getting farther and farther away, but all she wanted to do was slump down. She glanced wearily back to the shore to see how far they'd come.

And found, to her horror, that she couldn't see it.

It was hidden behind a bank of white cloud. No, not cloud. Fog. And it was rolling towards them across the black ice, moving fast.

'Evan!'

'What?' He didn't even bother to turn around.

The fog was coming at an incredible speed. Dense and white, moving like a tsunami wave. She turned and began to run towards him.

'Look behind you. That's not good, is it?'

She grabbed his hand and spun him round. He gasped. It was closing in on them, rolling closer and closer. Blotting out the sky, blotting out everything as though it was eating the world up.

'Lettie never said anything about fog,' he said.

She could hear the fear in his voice. Instinctively, despite their anger, they clutched at each other's hands as the leading edge ate up the last few metres and engulfed them. It was like suddenly going snow-blind. There was nothing but white. She couldn't see Evan, she couldn't even see herself.

'Don't let go,' said Evan's voice, faint even though he was next to her. 'Or we're lost. We stay still until it . . .'

His voice had faded out.

'Evan!' she shouted, but her voice went nowhere. All she could feel was his hand holding hers.

She grasped it tighter. Nothing would make her let go. But what she grasped was empty air. She tried again, but her hand was empty. She felt around, desperately.

He was gone.

Somehow he'd managed to slip away from her hand. Panic swept over her. He'd done it on purpose! He'd left her. She spun round and shouted, but all that came out was a dead-flat whisper. She ran a few steps and stopped, her heart pounding.

Something touched her.

'Evan?'

No answer. But a shadow loomed ghostly in front of her. No! Several shadows. Weird shapes, like grotesque birds, or monsters with plumes on their heads. Shadows moved and twisted like giant wings stirring the thick fog. She was surrounded.

Now someone was standing in front of her. Someone tall. A face formed out of the mist. It came into focus. Black hair, icy skin, silver eyes. She turned to run, but a woman was there behind her, black hair, silver eyes, skin like ice. She caught Nell in her arms.

'Feldmar, take her!' the woman commanded.

There was a smell like hot metal. A great hook grabbed her shoulders in a fierce grip. A huge wind tore at her, then stopped. Her head thudded painfully, as though someone had hit her with a cricket bat, then her ears popped. The fierce wind tore round her again, and stopped. She hadn't been hit. She was going up into the air – fast. She felt down with her foot but there was no ground beneath her now. The surge of wind came again. Another rush of blood to her head, her ears popped. She was being dragged up higher. She screamed but no sound came. The tears on her face froze and the breath in her lungs turned to ice.

I'm dying, she thought, and passed out.

Thirteen

Nell opened her eyes. Her heart gave a thump. She was alive at least. She looked around. She was on her own. The room was in twilight, like everywhere else in this ice world.

For a moment she could only stare blankly, unable to work out where she was. Then it rushed back to her.

I was surrounded by freaky creatures. Then something took me up high. I fainted. And now I'm inside.

She sat up, her breath smoking. It was no warmer in here than outside. She was lying on a mattress made of something soft and warm, probably goose feathers, covered with a quilt that was throwing out heat. She could feel her body thawing out from some extreme cold. Even in the goose gloves and boots her fingers and toes felt frozen. She wanted to stay in the warmth of the bed, but she couldn't. She got up, rubbing her sore shoulders where the iron hook had grasped her, and tiptoed to a frosted window. She rubbed until she could see through. Outside the lake stretched to the horizon, where the Mother Harp pierced the sky.

I'm in one of the palaces, she realized. Either the Thorns or Stones saw us.

But where was Evan? She remembered their hands slipping apart. Had they taken him, too, or was he still free? Staring out of the window in this cold, bare room wouldn't answer any of her questions. She had to find out. She tiptoed over to the door and listened.

Somewhere there was drumming, loud drumming, like when the music teacher got all the hand drums out at school, the bongos, tablas and bodhráns, and they sat in a circle and drummed to different rhythms as though they'd slipped back to tribal times. Over and around it people were shouting. Something squawked, high-pitched and angry. A great roar of laughter went up. She peered out. The noise was coming from the other end of a corridor that ended in a wide and tall archway. She could see people moving about beyond it.

It sounded like a party, with people enjoying themselves.

Steeling herself, her hands screwed into tight fists, she took a deep breath, and keeping to the wall, she crept towards the arch. When she reached it, she flattened herself against the wall and edged along, until she could lean round and peek inside.

Straight away the noise level dropped.

'Come in,' shouted a voice.

Were these Thorns or Stones? And how much did they hate humans? Giving herself no time to worry further, she stepped through the arch and into a huge banqueting hall.

It was the size of Westminster Abbey. It stretched out before her, packed with Elven, the ceiling so high it almost disappeared into a haze of smoke. She gazed up and up into the rafters and saw that the owner of the harsh shriek was glaring down at her. He wasn't alone, about ten great lammergeyers were perched on the huge beams and fighting over scraps of fish, before swooping down again for more. Evan hadn't exaggerated when he said the lake lammergeyers were bigger. They were three times the size of a man. The smell of hot metal wafted over her.

She walked forward. Either side there were long tables and a space in the middle where fish, meat and baskets of shellfish were being roasted over an open fire. It was the only heat in the place. Everyone was in the snow goose suits, but in lots of different designs. They weren't all like hers, black, grey and white. Some had been dyed bright colours, so that here and there spots and splashes of crimson and peacock blue stood out. Some had feather decorations, and plumes on the hoods. A few were all black and forbidding. So these were the weird monsters she'd seen outlined in the fog. Not monsters but Ice Elven being fashionable in their own way.

She kept walking and looking, trying to keep herself calm and not panic. It might be important to know where everything was, if she was going to get away. Over in one corner a group of boys were playing an assortment of drums, pleasing themselves, bashing away happily. Her music teacher would have liked the sound they made. Everyone else was eating, or cooking, or shouting at each other. Little children were running around in fur and feather outfits, like polar bear cubs, doing normal little kid stuff, like fighting or chasing each other, or laughing at two lammergeyers who were fighting over a bone.

It was like a Viking feast. As she walked along, the Ice Elven looked at her, and some smiled, some turned away, but no one made her feel like running. She'd thought their palaces would be silent and frozen and grim. Not loud with music and feasting.

There was a great gale of laughter, and she flinched as a lammergeyer nearly knocked her over as it took off from beside her, its wings pounding the air. She'd never been so close to one. It took her breath away; its feathers looked like beaten bronze as they reflected the firelight. She'd seen them in the forest that first time, dropping bones from heights. Evan called them bone breakers. She'd googled them when she got back and found that in her world lammergeyers were big birds, like vultures, who lived on marrowbones and who were fond of dropping tortoises from heights to crack them open. But Ice Elven lammergeyers were the size of a hang-glider. No wonder the one that was flapping its wings and taking off beside her could lift up the Elven boy who was hanging beneath it, held tightly by the bird's giant claws. The boy shouted with excitement as the bird rose vertically and then flew to the other end of the hall with him, leaving behind a strong gust of hot metal. It was the same smell she'd noticed before she'd been kidnapped.

Nell hugged her shoulders and shivered. So that's what had gripped her shoulders – not an iron hook, but a Lammergeyer's claw. That's how they'd brought her here, dangling beneath a giant bird. Thank goodness for the fog, so she hadn't known.

The lammergeyer was flying back now, and it released the laughing boy from its claws. He dropped and landed a few metres from Nell.

Loki!

211

He stopped laughing when he saw her. Nell couldn't tell what he was thinking. He might have been glad to see her, at their mercy like this. Or he might have been angry she'd dared to cross the lake after he'd tried to stop her.

He glanced sideways at a table. From out of the smoke and the sea of faces watching them, she spotted Laki straight away. She was wearing an all-white snow suit. She looked amazing as usual, but her face was moody, her chair tipped back, and she was twirling a goblet round in her hands as though she'd like to throw it. She looked like Gwen when things weren't going her way.

'I warned you not to come,' she said.

'Never mind that,' a voice shouted. 'Bring her over here!'

Loki pushed her forward. An Ice Elven was lounging in a throne-like seat. She recognized his outfit from the fog. And the woman sitting next to him.

So I get to meet Loki and Laki's parents, she thought. Because there was no mistaking it. The family resemblance was remarkable. Nell stood in front of them, with Loki and Laki on either side, and had no idea what to say.

'I give my children one job to do, and they fail,' said their father.

There was no mistaking that he and their mother were

the bosses round here. The other Ice Elven who were sitting close by were watching and waiting to see what would happen, without interfering.

'Sit.' The woman pointed to a chair, but Nell ignored her.

Laki bit her lip. 'Sit, Nell. Don't be stubborn.'

She shook her head. 'They kidnapped me, against my will.'

The man raised his eyebrows. He didn't look totally displeased at her answer.

'Unstiffen, human. Learn how to have fun.' He swept his arm round at all the noise and laughter. 'This is how to live properly. Get used to it, you'll be here a long time.'

He had the same silver eyes as Loki and Laki, and he was staring, trying to make her look away, but she refused.

'I was living before you trapped me in the fog,' she said.

He raised an eyebrow. 'It's a good trick, isn't it? Useful for hunting.'

Loki moved suddenly, and appeared behind her. He pushed down hard on her shoulders, and she had to sit down in the seat next to Laki. She wanted to hit him, but then she saw him ducking as one of the huge birds flew past at low level. If he hadn't made her sit she would've got knocked down anyway.

Unlikely as it seemed, Loki had saved her from a bruising.

'Careful of the birds,' said his mother. 'They can be dangerous, but they're better than flitting. More stylish.'

'We train them like humans train hawks for hunting,' said Loki. They both had the same sly smile, mother and son. 'One carried you here. You fainted from the cold. Are you getting warmer?'

'Uh-huh.' Her fingers were beginning to thaw out and her toes were aching as the goose-down-lined boots heated up her feet again.

'Drink this.' Loki put a goblet down in front of her. It steamed. 'It's not poisoned.'

She took a sip. It tasted like chocolate mixed with chilli. She drank it quickly and felt it burning a path down to her stomach. It acted like an energy drink. It sharpened her mind and she began to look round and take notice of things.

'What are you thinking?' said Loki.

'The Vikings in our world had a place called Valhalla, where the warriors went when they died. I think it might have looked like this.'

'Glad you like it. You'll be stopping. I did warn you.'

'I won't be stopping. Where's Evan?'

He shrugged. 'We don't know. He's a sly one, not bad

for a Forest Elven. They tend to be dull and slow.'

The Elven slow? thought Nell. What must they think of humans?

'You mean he got away.'

Loki nodded. 'He did.'

'So let me go. I need to find him.'

'Listen.'

The noise in the hall stopped so suddenly that it almost made her dizzy. Even the Lammergeyers stopped squawking and flapping. The ground began to tremble beneath her feet. Her ears popped. Then it began – the terrible harp screech, echoing down the ice passages and filling the hall to the rafters. Nell cringed and counted.

Seven seconds!

Her heart began to thud. The harps were dying too fast. There was no time to sit at a feast. Then an awful thought hit her.

Or maybe there was all the time in the world.

Loki was watching her. 'You gambled and lost, Nell. Admit it.'

She was glad he'd said it. If Loki thought he'd won, then she would fight to her last breath.

I haven't lost yet, she told him, silently. Not till the end. Her dad said she was like a pit bull. She might look skinny but she was tenacious.

'You shouldn't have come. You're stuck here. Get used to it.'

She thumped the table. 'I can't believe you're sitting here, having a feast, whilst the world is dying. DYING!' she shouted. Everyone stopped and listened. 'Are you all crazy? Let me find Evan and we'll start the harps again.'

Loki looked unimpressed by her outburst. 'No.'

'Do you want to die? Or do you think you can all come through to our world at the last moment? Because, really, I don't see you fitting in.'

Loki laughed. 'If we came to your world we wouldn't fit in. We'd take it off you.'

'I don't think so. Fen has already tried that and failed.'

Laki suddenly jumped to her feet. 'Oh for Krake's sake! Tell her the truth!'

Loki's father waved a hand to shut his daughter up. 'She's right. You have a right to know. You've fought hard, I admire that. Now find out why you should have stayed away.'

A silence fell, first those around the table going silent, then it spread to the other tables. A few Elven wandered over to listen. Loki's father leaned across the table to Nell.

'When the harps stop we have a plan. The ice lake will not die like the rest of the Elven world. We will float free for the first time, free of the human world that we've been tethered to. And free of the other Elven. Just ice and the Ice Elven.'

'How it should be,' said his mother. 'We'll grow a new world from this lake, one that works how we want it.'

Nell frowned. 'That sounds impossible.'

Loki waved a casual hand. 'Krake, our Vanir, will do it.'

Nell turned to him. 'The one who left Aurora and the others?'

He nodded. 'Left the traitor gods who went to live with the humans.'

She stood up. 'Let me speak to him.'

What was she saying? Speak to a god, make him change his mind? Yeah, right. But she'd spoken to the Vanir in her world. She and Evan had stood up to them. They'd got what they wanted. It might be possible.

But they were all laughing at her now.

'You want to meet Krake?' said Loki. 'I don't think you'd survive long.'

'OK. So let me go. I'll turn round. I'll find Evan. The Rivers family can come and live in my world. You don't have to keep me here.'

Loki's father laughed, harshly. 'Humans share the world? I don't think so.'

She whirled round to Laki. 'Tell them,' she cried.

'We're not all like that! It could work. We could share.'

Laki said nothing for a moment, then she banged her goblet down. 'She's right! Let her go.' She looked defiantly at her mother and father. 'I liked the human world, actually. There's not that much difference between us and them. *Or* us and the other Elven.'

Her mother drew in a breath. 'Stop being ridiculous.' She reached forward to slap her but Laki was too quick and jumped up beside Nell.

'It's true,' she snapped. 'So just let her go.'

'Please,' said Nell eagerly. 'I'll find Evan. We'll leave. We'll go back to my world. We won't bother you any more.'

'See?' Laki glared at her mother and father. 'She's sickeningly honest. She'll keep her word. Let her go.'

Loki tipped his chair back and grinned. 'Laki likes the human,' he chanted. He seemed to be enjoying this.

Laki tossed her hair back, and for a moment she looked like Gwen again, beautiful and determined to get her own way, whatever any adult thought. She fixed her father with a Gwen-like princess stare. 'You told us humans were either evil or stupid. They aren't.'

Her father looked furious, but in the same way that Tom looked mad when Gwen cheeked him. They were men who could rule others, but when it came to their

218

daughters getting all moody and snappy, they couldn't handle it.

'You were tricked by them, Laki,' was all he managed to say. 'Humans would kill us all in the blink of their coloured eyes. We need to be separate. Stupid girl.'

This made Laki look even more dangerous.

'Actually, I've been thinking,' she said. 'Going off and making a world all of our own will be boring. There'll be no one to fight with. No one to make jokes about. Just us and Krake, and he's no fun. He's all anger and taboos and bow-down-to-me-or-else.'

The sound of indrawn breaths came from all around. Most of the Ice Elven had stopped and were watching. Nell took a swift look around. The older ones didn't seem pleased at what they were hearing, but the younger ones were wriggling through the gaps in the crowd and moving closer, eagerly, as though they might shout out in support.

Laki turned on her brother. 'Tell them. You mixed with the humans as well. You enjoyed it, I know you did.'

Loki grinned. 'Because I played with their minds.'

His sister's answering grin was just as sly. 'That's why Nell got to you, because you couldn't twist her mind.'

Loki cast Nell a quick, angry glance. 'I despise her as I despise all humans.'

Laki laughed. 'You don't. You admire bravery as much as any Ice Elven.'

Loki managed to get his mocking smile back.

'Mother,' he said, pretending to be scared. 'Tell Laki, she's caught human germs. She's having doubts.'

Two girls, around her age, jumped forward. 'Shut up, Loki. Laki's right. It will be boring.'

Then a boy pushed through to them. 'I want to go and see the human world,' he said eagerly. 'Send me, I'll tell you what it's really like.'

Laki's parents were furious.

'We've made a pact with the Stones,' her mother shouted. 'Now shut up!'

'Who cares what the Stones say?' Laki shouted back. 'We're the Thorns, we can do what we want. Imagine being stuck for all eternity with the Stones. Old Harald Stone smells.'

And with that, everyone started crowding round and shouting and arguing. Laki's parents jumped up and joined in, but they could hardly be heard. Laki laughed in delight at the mayhem she'd caused. She moved out of the fray and caught Nell's eye. She gave a wink and then nodded towards a door behind their table.

Nell nodded back, and waited whilst Laki turned round and began to fuel the argument by jumping on to the table and stamping her feet and demanding her parents listen to the young Elven, and not some old god.

Her mother and father were furious. Her mother tried to slap her leg, but Laki began skipping up and down the table, knocking over the goblets and kicking platters of meat to the floor. Everyone was watching her – some cheering, some shouting at her to stop.

No one was watching Nell. She stepped back, out of the way.

Look no one in the eye, shrink down, hunch your shoulders. This is what she did at school if she didn't want to be noticed. It worked there and it worked here.

She wandered away. Cease to catch people's eye. Cease to be interesting. Blend in. Camouflage. Move like you're going nowhere, drift off. Don't make any sudden or suspicious movements that catch people's attention. Take an interest in the sculpture standing by the door.

She ran her hand over the strange carving that stood taller than a man.

Was it made of walrus tusk? And what was it supposed to be? A sea creature perhaps. Lettie said something lived under the ice. Maybe it was this. It looked like a sea serpent with a long neck and straggling hair like a mermaid. She ran her hand over it and then let it wander to the door frame. She was nearly outside.

One tiny last glance back. For a moment she thought Loki had spotted her, but he turned away and started shouting at Laki again, instead of raising the alarm, so he couldn't have. She found herself in a corridor, and sauntered along it until she rounded a corner and no one could see her. Then she ran. Halfway along a gust of wind hit her. It was coming from an open door. She glimpsed a view of the outside, the lake stretching away into the distance.

A few more steps and she was through it and running like she'd never run before. The wind buffeted and pushed at her, and her tears froze again. She blinked them away and they fell like little icicles.

She took one look back and saw the palace for the first time, all sharp spires with the great hall dominating everything. There were arches high up, just below its roof – for the lammergeyers to fly from, she presumed. None were leaving. None had been told to fetch her.

The black ice was clear of fog. She whirled round and tried to work out how far they'd brought her, but the only landmark was the black needle of the Mother Harp. It was still distant, but slightly closer. She began walking, she would make for that and hope Evan was doing the same. As she left the shadow of the palace, she was surprised to see that it had been built close to a harp. It loomed over her, thick as a redwood tree and high enough for its top to be shrouded in cloud. It was not as big as the ones in the forest with their hundred cables, but big enough. She curved left to give it a miss. She'd seen the dead birds near the others, and that was before they began dying. If it made its screeching, dying wail when she was underneath it, she'd probably be deafened or sent mad.

She began to run, and in her mind's eyes she saw herself from the lammergeyers' viewpoint again – a tiny goose-feathered dot fleeing across an endless expanse of shining black. She checked again for the great birds, but if she'd been looking down at her feet, not up at the purple sky, then she might have noticed that not all the ice was black here. Suddenly her foot hit something that cracked beneath it. She tripped and fell to her knees.

The ice below her was white and creaking. She tried to scramble to her feet, but another crack tore across the delicate white surface. No, spread your weight, she told herself in a panic. It's like quicksand. But as fast as her thought was, the ice was faster.

It shattered beneath her like a car windscreen, and she fell straight down into the black water below.

Fourteen

It had happened. Her worst nightmare.

She dropped like a stone through the black water, in a shroud of fizzing bubbles.

Her ears popped as she plunged downwards, and then she felt her descent slow and stop. For a second or two she hung in the water in total silence, her eyes squeezed shut. So far she hadn't frozen to death. The goose suit was keeping out the water. Her face had gone numb, though.

Move, you idiot! her brain screamed. Get to the surface, cling to the edge of the ice, then pull yourself out.

Don't think of what might be below you!

She reached her arms above her head and swam manically upwards, pulling and kicking wildly. Two strokes, three strokes, four, five. How deep had she plunged?

She wanted to breathe. No, not yet, the screaming voice insisted.

Seven . . . eight strokes. She must be nearly at the surface. But something smacked down on her head and she sank again. For a moment she couldn't think what had happened. Had someone hit her with a cricket bat? No, it was the other way round. She'd hit something. There was ice above her!

She'd missed the hole. The horror of it froze her mind.

She scrabbled around, feeling the rutted ice above her, knowing that it was metres thick. She pushed frantically with her hands, a trickle of icy water leaking into the suit and freezing her skin. But how was she going to crack metres of solid ice? All she did was push herself down into the freezing blackness.

Panic swept over her and whirled her mind into a shrieking terror-filled babble. *I'm dying, I'm drowning, trapped, can't breathe, I'm dead . . .*

And then the trickle of icy water into the goose suit became an explosion, as the insulation became waterlogged. It was so sudden, so cold, she thought her heart had stopped. Maybe it has, she thought wildly. Maybe she'd frozen solid in an instant. But it jolted her mind out of its whirlpool of terror.

No! Stop and think! Look around.

She opened her eyes. Blackness everywhere, except for a grey circle on the surface that was rapidly moving away from her, as the current pulled her viciously away. Her cheeks bulged desperately with the last breath she'd taken before she'd fallen.

How long did a breath last – a minute? Two minutes at most? *Oh Lord, she was going to die – underwater.*

No. Think!

The only sound was the beating of her own heart. It was loud and close up, like when a car stops next to you at traffic lights and they've got the bass turned up really loud so that its muffled thump hits you in the chest. *Boom . . . boom . . . boom.*

I'm still alive. Think.

Something touched her foot. She let out a scream that sounded like something coming out of headphones, tinny and distant, and taking away part of her precious last breath. The something touched her again and wrapped round her ankle. She flapped and kicked in pure panic until she saw amongst the bubbles fizzing around her a strand of weed go bobbing past her eyes. She glanced down fearfully, and saw shadows waving in the dark water. Waterweed, that's all, blowing about in the current.

Get away from it. Don't get tangled. Forget breathing. Concentrate. Think of how to get out. Look around.

Fear had pumped adrenaline through her body. It kicked in and she scanned around. Blackness, that's all. Apart from over to her left, a blacker line amidst a dark grey patch. There was something enormous going down into the depths and reaching up to the surface as well. And surrounding it on the surface was a patch of lighter grey. Her heart gave a big boom as she realized what it was.

She was looking at the massive black column of the harp she'd passed before she fell. It was directly opposite her now as she got tugged backwards. If she swam towards it she'd be going sideways to the current. Her dad had told her that was the way to beat a rip tide at sea. Always swim sideways to the pull of the water, he'd said. She began to swim towards it, and he was right. This time she was making headway. She could feel herself moving forwards with each pull of her arms.

She kept her eyes fixed on that dim circle of grey where the harp left the water. The harps vibrated when they made music. Vibrations caused heat, that's why people shivered when they got cold. And heat melts ice. That little grey circle around the column of the harp was melted ice. And she was closing on it. She pulled at the water, clawing at it, trying to streamline her body like a dolphin inside the soaking clothes. Second by second she was edging closer to the harp, but she was in agony now. Her lungs were screaming to breathe.

They yearned. They ached, they nagged, they insisted. The desire to breathe became overwhelming.

Breathe and you're dead, she told herself. You can do two lengths of the swimming pool underwater, easily. All you have to do is keep calm. Don't panic. Believe your heart has slowed or stopped, you don't need air.

She remembered Evan saying that the Ice Elven could survive because their hearts beat so slow. She was so frozen now she couldn't feel her body at all. No use pumping oxygen round a frozen body. The bass boom of her heart began to slow.

Now swim! She was good underwater. Half a length of the baths and she'd reach the harp, that's all.

She felt her heart slow further. Until something touched her foot again!

A streamlined shape swam past her at high speed. She caught a flash of silver scales – a big fish, that's all. Don't think of it! Survive.

The black column grew clearer, looming out of the darkness, huge and terrifying as it plunged into the depths.

Head for that. Swim upwards, never mind that the goose suit was heavy and waterlogged and dragging her down. She pulled mightily with her arms. Two, three, four strokes. She was going upwards. The grey circle was growing. The column of the harp was moving rapidly towards her, covered in barnacles and short black weeds like dead people's hair. She banged against it and heard it gong dully. But it gave her something to kick against and she shot upwards at speed. And now there was another sound gonging in her ears. Not the metal clang of the column, or the slow bass beat of her heart. Something else. Like a voice shouting from a long way above her. She dragged at the water with her frozen arms, but the suit was so heavy. She looked up in despair and thought she saw a face leaning over the edge of the grey line, shouting and screaming. The muffled noise spurred her on once more, but then it was drowned out by fizzing.

Bubbles were bursting all around her, popping in her eyes, tickling her face. What was happening? Why were bubbles rising up around her? What was beneath her?

She looked down. She shouldn't have. Something was rising from the deep. And it was rising fast. She began to kick frantically for the surface, but she couldn't stop herself taking another glance.

A face!

It was looming up from the depths, human or devil she

couldn't tell, but scaled like a snake. The creature in the lake. Long hair writhed round it and billowed out, like strands of weed. A long hand with curved nails appeared, reaching for her feet.

No way.

She kicked out madly. Don't think of it! Survive, that's all. Swim or else that thing will grab your feet and pull you down for ever.

She kicked like crazy and the water turned into a giant Slush Puppie, grey and gelid, half liquid, half frozen. She began to scrabble at it, rising fast, kicking to keep herself up. Then someone was scrabbling at it from the other side, from above. Something was reaching out towards her. It was a hand.

She thrust her own frozen fingers up through the slush and touched it, but she was too numb with cold to grasp. It didn't matter. The hand grasped hers. She felt herself being pulled upwards through the crackling slush.

There was air on her face, but she was too frozen to breathe.

'Kick, Nell.'

She flailed feebly with her legs and felt something graze her heel as she bent her knees and pulled her feet free of the water. Someone pulled her hard and she felt herself slide out on to the ice like a baby seal. It was Evan, soaking wet too. She got a quick glimpse of his face before he hit her in the chest.

'Breathe,' he ordered.

Easy to say, but here she was in the air, lying on the ice next to the towering harp, and she couldn't. Her chest had frozen. Her lungs were blocks of ice. She felt herself being lifted and thrown down on to her front. Then there was a pressure on her back. A huge thump.

Evan had rescued her and now he was killing her. Another huge thump made her jolt and lift off the ice and then fall back down. And again. Now something was coming out of her mouth. It was black freezing water mixed with chips and shards of ice.

And suddenly he'd stopped the thumping and she'd got herself up on her hands and knees and she was drawing in a huge breath, and it was so painful, but so amazing all at the same time. And then it wheezed out of her. And she took another, less painfully this time. And another, and she was breathing and gasping like she'd run a marathon. She was still frozen and about to die of frostbite, but she was breathing and it was sweet. She sat down on the ice with a thump and leaned against the black column of the harp and looked back at him. He was watching her, his stricken face gradually relaxing.

No, don't relax!

Because Nell could see something happening behind him. The slushy water was churning and something was climbing out. It was the thing she'd seen racing up towards her in the water. Except now it was slithering across the ice, its scales shining dully, half sea serpent, half Elven, with long hair dragging and dripping from its scaly neck. It was stalking towards Evan, creeping across the ice like a lizard, its fanged mouth gaping, its eyes pinned on him.

Nell tried to shout. She tried to warn him. Her mouth wouldn't work. She couldn't even point, her arms were frozen. She could only watch in horror as it rose up behind him, hissing and dribbling water that froze instantly into a beard of icicles. Evan heard and turned, but it was too late. It lashed out and in the blink of an eye it had wrapped a claw round his leg.

Terror swept over Evan's face. He tried to clutch the ice with his nails as the creature dragged him backwards.

Nell found her voice. 'No. Leave him!'

She tried to fling herself forward but her legs were rubber and didn't belong to her. Their eyes met for a moment. And then the creature heaved and Evan slid over the edge, and disappeared below the ice.

Fifteen

He was gone.

She knelt there, stunned and silent. A wind had picked up and was blowing around her, freezing her soaking wet clothes. She knew it was killing her but she couldn't move. She couldn't think.

Evan was beneath the ice. The creature had him. And she could do nothing. There was no clever plan, no act of bravery that could change this and make it better.

'No,' she said, her voice tiny.

She tried to stand but fell over, and tried again and failed. In the end she slithered towards the hole on her knees. She looked down into the still black water. She'd stopped shivering now. She was way beyond shivering. She was a piece of ice. And Evan was gone.

'No!' She screamed it this time, making the column

235

of the harp sing slightly. 'No, no, no, that can't have happened!'

'Yes. It did. Unfortunately.'

It was Aurora's voice, as cold and unfeeling as the ice.

Nell managed to turn her head, her frozen neck creaking. The Vanir was standing beside Nell, tall and gaunt, her marble skin shining like frost in the dim light, her tattered ragbag clothes blowing in the killer wind. And behind her was Arn, clad in ice-trimmed leathers, his face like thunder, looking her up and down with distaste, but pity as well.

The most ferocious anger she had ever felt welled up inside her. If Aurora and Arn hadn't been sulking cowards, leaving the world they'd created to fall to pieces, then Evan wouldn't be dying below her feet in a freezing, suffocating hell.

'It was Krake, wasn't it?' she screamed at Aurora. 'That thing with the scales and the seaweed hair and the lizard claws. That's their god.'

'Yes.'

The other Vanir, the one who'd argued and left them. The one who was going to make the Ice Elven a new world.

'Don't just stand there,' Nell shouted. 'You're gods – go and get Evan back. Now!'

Instead of jumping straight into the water, Aurora stared at her. 'We saw. We were just too late.'

'Living underwater hasn't improved him,' said Arn, inches away from her face now.

If she had had any feeling left in her body she would've jumped back in fright. But moving any of her limbs wasn't an option for her now. The killer wind was doing its job well and killing her. Both she and Evan, dead on the lake. Some rescue team they had turned out to be.

No, she mustn't think like that. She was Nell, she was a pit bull terrier. She couldn't give up until she keeled over.

'Go fetch Evan back,' she shouted at Aurora, except that her voice came out as a weak croak. For some reason she wanted to yawn and go to sleep. 'There's time. I nearly froze. I nearly died. But I lived.'

Aurora folded her arms and looked her up and down. 'Not for long. You're dying now. Of cold.'

The next moment Arn put his creaking leather-clad arms around her and hugged her tight in a big bear grip.

'Get off me,' she managed to whimper. 'You sick person.'

Arn's arms didn't budge. She could hardly breathe.

'Stupid human. I'm trying to warm you,' he rumbled impatiently in her ear.

'I just want you to save Evan,' she gasped, as she felt the first glimmer of heat pierce through the frozen goose feathers.

'I'm going,' said Aurora. 'I will find Krake. You concentrate on not freezing to death.'

She slipped into the slushy water as though she'd entered a hot spa on a sunny day. Her head sank, her hair briefly blossoming out like weed, and she was gone.

Nell tried to look down, to see if she could see Evan. Maybe he'd got away from Krake? But Arn held her too tightly. She couldn't move. And now the little trickle of heat had become fiercer. Somehow Arn was swamping her in warmth. Every part of her goose suit began to steam. And she began to shiver so hard she thought her teeth would shatter and her eyes fall out.

'Shivering is good,' she heard Arn say. 'It means you're not dying any more. Possibly.' He gave a cruel snigger. 'Soon, when your blood starts to flow again, you might wish you'd died.'

She didn't know what he meant until the pain started. First her toes and fingers, then it spread like wildfire. Hot aches, her mum called it. When you come in out of the cold and sit by the fire and your toes and fingers start to ache like mad. Except that this time her whole body had hot aches, from her toes to the roots of her hair. Tiny blood vessels that had clamped shut to allow the little remaining warm blood to keep her brain alive were warming up and opening as her blood defrosted and began to flow again.

She squeezed her eyes shut and endured, not daring to think about how many minutes had passed since Evan had disappeared beneath the water. But at last the pain subsided and she opened her eyes and found herself still cradled by Arn.

'Is he back?' she said. She'd stopped shivering.

'No.'

She hardly dared ask, but she had to know. 'How long has it been?'

'Who knows. Many minutes?'

No, no, no, no, no.

Incredibly she was nearly dry. She could feel the feathers in her suit lifting and becoming light and airy again.

'That creature, that thing,' she stammered.

Arn stared moodily down into the water. 'Krake. Our lost friend.'

'Monster. Some god he is. A devil more like. Why is he trying to kill Evan?'

Arn shrugged, as though it was plain to see. 'To stop him getting to the Mother Harp.'

Life came back into her limbs, a desperate, despairing energy. She pushed her way out of his arms and looked down. Nothing. No movement from the hole. No sign of Aurora or Evan. How long could Elven hold their breath?

'Then he's a murderer.'

'No.'

'Why isn't Aurora stopping him?'

'She's trying.'

'But Evan's dying under there,' she cried.

'No.'

She really wanted to hit Arn, to pummel his chest with her fists. 'Shut up saying no! He's been under for too long. Longer than me and I was nearly dead.'

Arn stared into the distance as though she hadn't spoken. 'They're fighting,' he said, as though receiving a telepathic message.

Immediately, a few metres away, something thumped the ice from below. Nell whirled round. The thump came again. She saw the ice jolt upwards slightly, and crack like a thunderclap. She ran towards it, not knowing what it was, or even if it was safe. At least it was something, some movement from below. Beneath her feet a network of little cracks was running and spreading. She fell to her knees and began to brush the layer of frost from the ice surface. The black glass beneath her cleared.

There! Deep below she could see movement. It was the scaly head and trailing hair of Krake. She brushed more frost away. And there beside him – the white face of Evan. Aurora was swirling round them, as though trying to stop Krake taking Evan further away.

It was terrible. Like watching a horror movie but it was real. She thumped on the ice with her fist.

'Hey, let him go!'

She stood up and jumped up and down, screaming, hardly daring to look at Evan's blurred face, white against the black water. Once she'd been scared of ice cracking, now all she wanted to do was shatter it.

Then Krake had broken free of Aurora's circling and they were moving through the water again. She ran after them, kicking the frost layer away to reveal Evan's pale face beneath the ice, as Krake dragged him and Aurora followed. Then she lost him again, and she ran about madly, dropping to her knees and brushing the frost away, finding nothing and running to another spot, looking and looking. Minutes ticked by. Surely ten minutes had passed? She wanted to slump down and cry but she couldn't give up.

There was a loud crack again. And she saw Krake's body hit the ice from below as though Aurora had started to fight him. The water beneath the ice became a maelstrom of bubbles and whiteness. She could hear the Vanir roaring at one another below her feet. But what was happening to Evan whilst they fought? Where was he? What if they got carried away fighting and forgot about him and he sank down and down into that inky blackness? Never to be found again.

She jumped up and down. She screamed. She knelt down and thumped her fist against the ice. But they took no notice, and Krake broke free and she saw Evan's face, and felt relief, but only for a moment. She ran, following him, as he was dragged along, hanging limply from Krake's hand, like a puppet.

They stopped again; she jumped up and down, she kicked the ice.

'You're killing him!' she sobbed. He'd been down there too long. His blood would be frozen. His face stared up at her, blurred but still. His mouth was open. He wasn't holding his breath. No one could hold their breath that long.

'You monster. You idiots. You're not gods. You're killers.'

Arn must have been following her, because his arms wrapped round her again.

'Stop. You'll hurt yourself.'

What did he care? She flung her head back and caught

him on his chin. Then dragged her boot down his shinbone. He didn't even twitch. His arms still held fast around her.

'Come back. It's nearly over.'

He dragged her back to the harp, to the hole, and beneath their feet she could see Aurora and Krake swimming that way too. Aurora jumped out of the water like an Olympic swimmer, icicles forming immediately as she shook herself like a dog. But just as quickly they fell away and she began to dry.

Oh right, use god powers now, thought Nell, bitterly, as Arn held her. But not to save Evan.

And then that thing, that scaled creature with the Elven face and the long seaweed hair, leaped out. He was carrying Evan, still and white, and laying him down as though he was a rubber figure.

Arn let her go and she fell to her knees beside him. She could hardly bear to look at him. She thought her own heart was going to shatter like ice. He was lying as still as marble. His skin was stone cold. His eyes and face covered with a layer of frost, growing thicker by the second.

'Warm him up!' she demanded.

He'd been under too long. But that was OK. She'd heard about this. He could be in hibernation.

'Too late,' said Aurora, casually.

243

Nell sprang to her feet. She wanted to hit Aurora for being so uncaring. But she had no chance. The Vanir were taking no notice of her or Evan now. Aurora and Krake were face to face, with Arn watching avidly from the side. Nell took a step back. The gods were going to fight. They looked as though they were about to murder each other. Good, because they'd murdered Evan.

'So this is what you've become,' Aurora spat. She gestured towards Nell. 'A human killer.'

Krake's hideous face snarled, as the purple sky turned his scales to mauve and indigo. 'Shut up, Aurora, I didn't know she was going to fall into the lake. I came as soon as I could.'

Nell gaped at Krake. 'You're saying you were trying to save me?'

He looked down at her, affronted. 'Did someone tell the human to talk to me?'

But Nell wasn't going to back down. She glared right back into his black eyes. 'Don't you dare go all high and mighty and godly,' she shouted. 'You killed Evan. You monster bastard hell spawn freak.'

He opened his mouth, his fangs glinting. 'Come here, human.'

He reached for her, but Aurora's fist suddenly lashed out, and she hit him hard round the head. 'Shut up,

Krake. She doesn't understand what you did.'

What did that mean? Nell knew exactly what he'd done, but she made herself calm down and breathe deeply.

'OK, can we stop arguing and just thaw Evan out?' she said, holding back a huge backlog of sobs that threatened to swamp her. 'It might work. Humans who fall in icy water sometimes go into hibernation. They can be revived.'

All three of them stared at her and then stared at Evan lying still as death on the ice. He was covered in frost from head to foot now, like a lolly from the freezer.

'Not an Elven,' said Aurora, in that same casual tone. 'He can't be brought back like that.'

'You don't know for sure! You don't know everything. Try.'

Aurora shook her head. 'No, his heart's stopped. Feel it if you don't believe me.'

Nell backed away. 'No.' She didn't want proof. 'But you're gods,' she pleaded. 'Do something right. He's got to save the world with me. So bloody well save him!'

She was aware of distant voices behind her, but she ignored them. Nothing mattered but Evan.

'Listen, human,' hissed Krake. 'He's gone to the ice.'

Nell had no idea what that meant. 'Why would you do

that to people who used to worship you?'

'To change him for the better,' he said, with a sly smile on his scaly face.

'It's murder.'

'It's not. He's blessed.'

'You're crazy,' she cried, slipping to one side and then recovering. 'All of you.'

But then she was slipping again, her feet unable to grip the ice. She fell to her knees and looked wildly around. The Vanir were stumbling, too. The ice had begun to shake beneath their feet. Everywhere had a blurred quality, like an out-of-focus photograph. Even Loki and Laki, who were running across the ice towards them, were falling and then picking themselves up.

Nell crawled to Evan's body. She didn't want to see Loki's gloating face as they ran up to her over the quaking ice.

'Oh, you found him,' she heard him say coolly, as the pressure built up around them.

She glared up at Loki, as he tried to keep on his feet. Behind him the harp was a blur.

'What are you doing here? Come to gloat?' she shouted. 'Or mad that I managed to sneak away?'

He bent down. 'You are so irritating, Nell. I let you get away.' So he *had* seen her. 'And then you go and fall through the ice. Stupid human.'

'See what all your plotting did. Look at him! Your god killed him.'

Loki looked puzzled and then, incredibly, he gave a sort of smile. Nell had no time to do anything about that, though. The ice was shaking harder now. And Laki was beside her, trying to pull her towards the harp.

'Get close to it,' she cried. 'Safer. Like being in the eye of a storm.'

'Wait. Take Evan as well.'

But Loki had got him by his lifeless hands and was dragging him along. They stood in a tight group next to the column of the harp. Instinctively they all crouched down and clutched their ears. Aurora didn't bother. She covered Evan's ears instead.

The harp began to shake, and then came the clashing, ear-bursting chord.

Nell fixed her eyes on Evan and counted the seconds.

Six seconds. The harp was dying.

But Evan twitched.

Sixteen

As the harp screech died, Nell fell to her knees beside Evan. She began trying to brush the frost from his face.

'I saw a sign of life,' she shouted.

She looked up, but none of them were taking any notice of her. They were in a group talking about the harp, the Vanir murmuring to each other and Laki pleading with them in a low voice she couldn't properly hear after the deafening screech. She knew what they were saying. Six seconds, that's all. The world was dying faster and faster.

But the harp didn't matter to her, not at this moment, nor did the Vanir. She didn't care about gods any more. They were as stupid as people.

Because of them, everything was dying. Evan, the world. Her, probably.

Only Loki was standing apart. He was a couple of

metres away and doing nothing but stare at her with a frown.

'Please,' she said. 'I saw him move. Help him.'

He came over and crouched down. She was afraid he would gloat. Or smile again. He was the last person in the world she should ask for help, but there was no one else.

He didn't gloat. He didn't sneer at her. 'He's not dead. That's what they were trying to tell you. He's gone to the ice.'

'What does that mean?' said Nell, as the words *he's not dead* echoed through her mind. She hardly dared believe it.

Loki started to help brush the frost away from Evan's clothes. 'He's one of us now.' Nell stared at him, unable to figure out what he was saying. 'It was Krake's way of stopping him getting to the harps. Look at him. He's thawing.'

She sat back on her heels. He was right. Evan's clothes had started to steam slightly. The frost on his face was retreating. She touched his cheek. It was ice cold but not hard like marble any more. His hair was still dark from the black water of the lake. She ran her fingers through it. No, it wasn't wet, it was drying fast but staying dark. She began to understand what Loki was telling her.

'You mean he's become an Ice Elven? Is that even possible?'

Loki grinned. 'Of course it is. It happened to us a long time ago. When we moved here from the forests, we were the same as Evan and the other Elven. We had to change.'

'But why would you ever want to live here?' said Nell. The lake was hideous and evil. She could still feel that icy water closing around her, and the black depths falling away beneath her.

'The great-families had a falling-out. They called it the conflict, but it was a war. In the end the Stones and the Thorns fled. They hated the other families and wanted nothing more to do with them. And the families left in the forest hated us.'

'So they came to this lake?'

'They couldn't flee into the human world because they hated you, too. The only place they had to go was here. They froze at first. They thought they were going to die. But Krake, the outlaw Vanir, was already here. He helped them. They found they could stand the cold, their hearts started beating slower and slower.'

'We call it *going to the ice*,' said Laki, bending down next to her and looking at Evan. 'And that has happened to Evan. A little quicker, but he's like us.'

As though he knew he was being talked about, Evan groaned. Nell clutched his hand. He was alive, that was all that mattered. But would he be the same? Would he still be Evan now he was Ice Elven?

'He's coming round. It'll take him a while,' said Laki. She took hold of Nell's arm. 'But this isn't going well. The gods are fighting.'

Nell looked up. Laki was right. Aurora and Arn were stalking round Krake. Out of the water, Krake looked even more horrific, with his hair drying and hanging in long twisted locks to below his waist, and the scales on his face and body gleaming in toxic colours like petrol spilled on a road.

He stamped his foot and the sound of ice cracking echoed across the lake.

'Aurora and Arn,' he jeered. 'My so-called friends. Sitting in the human world for years and years, like statues.'

Nell couldn't stand by any longer. She ran over to them and pointed at Krake. 'At least they weren't plotting to let this world die so that they could float off all alone. So they wouldn't have to share. That's so selfish.'

They ignored her.

'Of course we stayed in the human world,' spat Aurora. 'It was the only sensible thing to do. We were tired and sick from making the world. And after you left, we knew that coming back to this world would just mean more fighting. Between us we'd probably have blown this place sky-high long before now.'

Krake sneered, a horrible sight. 'You were scared of me. And now you come crawling back, weak like measly humans.'

'Yes, why did you come?' said Nell.

Aurora looked at her. 'You came to us, and we turned you away. When you were gone, we argued. Some of us said that we had forgotten we were Vanir. We were like gods, we had made a world. It was decided we should follow and try to help, however hard it was. Only Arn and I were strong enough to attempt it.' Her hand lashed out and she thumped Krake in the chest. 'And all we find is you – and you're still an aggressive, arrogant fool!'

Krake hit her back. 'You want to fight? Here? Now?'

Nell couldn't believe what she was hearing. It was like something you'd hear in her school, between two stupid gangs. She took a deep breath and strode forward until she was between Aurora and Krake. They towered above her on either side. At first she thought they hadn't even noticed her. Then they both looked down.

'So you're telling me that a long time ago you fell out with each other?' She swung round to Krake. 'And you went off in a strop?'

A lizardy tongue shot out of his mouth and he licked

253

his thin lips. 'You simplify things, human girl.'

'But that's the essence of it.'

Behind her, she heard Arn give a scoffing laugh. 'She's right.'

Krake ignored him and continued to glare at Nell. 'How dare you talk to us like this?'

Good question, thought Nell. She was shivering with fear now, not cold, but after seeing Krake pull Evan under the water, she'd got no respect for him at all.

'Because you're not my gods,' she said. 'Gods are only gods because people say they are. Otherwise they're just bullies and big-heads who think they can stomp around and do what they want.'

Someone touched her arm. It was Loki. Behind him she could see Laki leaning over Evan. Steam was still rising from his suit. He was still mending. Good. But if she didn't sort this out then it wouldn't matter if he'd survived.

'What?' she said to Loki.

'Be careful,' he whispered. 'Krake could kill you easily. Our parents are all scared of him.'

Nell shook him away. She had nothing to lose. 'You, you and you.' She swung round pointing at the Vanir one by one, leaving Krake till last, so she could fix her eyes on him. 'You've got to make peace with each other. Patch up your argument. Or we'll all be lost for ever. Out in the cold. Alone.'

The three Vanir stared at her. Krake made an angry move towards her. 'I told you to shut up and keep out of this,' he growled.

'You know, actually, she's right.'

It was Loki. He gave her a glance and then walked forward until he was looking up at Krake. Nell could see him quaking. Dissing a god. That was a big deal, even for a boy as conceited as him. He cleared his throat nervously.

'We've been going along with you, Krake. My parents are convinced it's the right thing to do. Split off. Stay apart. You've brainwashed us all. But just because you're a god, doesn't make you right.'

Krake began to hiss, his black lizardy eyes narrowed. Loki took a step back, then stood his ground and raised his chin.

'We shouldn't just believe you. We've got to think for ourselves. That's what I learned from Nell in the human world. You don't just go and believe what one person tells you. Nell was supposed to hate the Elven. But she didn't. She made her own mind up.'

Nell blinked in astonishment. Her eyes met Loki's. For the first time he wasn't mocking her, or trying to twist things his way. She went and stood next to him.

'He's right.'

'Too late,' said Krake. 'I changed the boy to Ice. He won't harmonize with a human any more. Like all Ice Elven he'll hate you.'

'Wrong.'

It was Evan. He was on his feet and leaning on Laki.

He came hobbling over to them. His white hair was darker, not black and feathery but darker than the Elven white. His eyes had a layer of frost over their charcoal darkness. No, not a layer of frost, thought Nell. His eyes have become silver.

She forgot the argument, forgot the fact that the world was ending, for that moment. She smiled at him.

'Hey,' she said, as casually as she could.

'Hey.'

He could speak, but here was the test. 'Do you know who I am?'

He tried to smile but his face was still frozen. 'No idea. Some human girl who I've never met.'

She laughed and held out her hand. He took it. 'Krake says we're not in harmony any more.'

Evan gave the Vanir a contemptuous glance. 'He's wrong.'

She nodded. 'Thought so.'

His eyes were pinned on hers. 'Don't ever fall through

the ice again. I saw you disappear. I came running. I had no idea where you were. I kept shouting into the hole near the harp hoping you'd hear.' He shook his head. 'You nearly died, helping us.'

She pulled a face as though it was nothing. 'I thought you *had* died.'

He put a hand to his face. 'So did I,' he said. 'My heart's not beating.' He tried to give a smile. 'So I'm dead or I've gone to the ice.'

Aurora came over. 'You're half and half. I got you back before Krake could turn you totally. So where do your feelings lie?'

He didn't hesitate. 'With my family of course. I still want to save the world.' He looked around at the other Vanir. 'Maybe we should all be half Ice Elven, half Forest Elven, then we wouldn't have to fight or be separate.'

'Maybe we should all be part human as well and then we wouldn't have to fight about who lives in which world,' Nell said.

That stunned the Vanir into silence.

Laki said, 'Visit their world, Krake, it's like nothing you've ever seen.'

Before he could speak the ice gave a shudder.

No one moved. Everyone waited. The dark bruise of the sky above them, the black ice, the Elven and her in the

257

goose-feather gear, the Vanir in their tattered clothes, untouched by the cold, their marble-like faces expressionless.

A quick glance at Krake showed he was smiling. Or what he took to be a smile, probably.

'It's beginning to come apart,' said Aurora. She turned to Krake. 'Is this what you want? To sail off with the Thorns and the Stones? To be apart for ever?'

'It's what he's been telling our parents since the harps started to fail,' said Loki. 'No one dares challenge him.'

The ice gave another shudder, and this time there were cracks and creaks from all around them.

It's dying around us, thought Nell, and we stand about not knowing what to do. Is this how it's going to end?

Aurora glided over to Krake and put her hand on his scaly frozen arm.

'Let them go to the harp. Let them try and restart it. Maybe it won't work, but they should try, the human and the Elven.'

'Like you did, all those centuries ago, with *him*,' said Krake, his monster face twisting.

I know that look, thought Nell. I know that tone of voice. I heard it last night when Gwen and Becca and Jake were cheating on each other.

Had the Vanir's argument stemmed from Krake and Aurora fighting about a human man?

'I loved him,' murmured Aurora, her voice like distant thunder.

'Huh,' said Krake.

'But it's over now. Let's forget. Let's heal the wound,' said Aurora. 'He's long gone.'

'Some gods we turned out to be,' said Arn. 'I agree with Aurora, let them try to restart the harps. If it works, then the Forest Elven can have their forest safe again. And the Ice Elven can keep their lake. If they want a separate world all for themselves, then I'm sure you, Krake, can spin it for them. Or you can go off on your own.'

Aurora didn't wait for Krake to say anything, she turned on her heel and said to Nell and Evan, 'Go, quickly.' Then she took a second look at Nell, grabbing her shoulders and staring deep into her eyes.

What now?

'You haven't much time. The Elven world's affecting you. The poisons are seeping into you.'

'I know. A day and a night. So let me go and do this.'

'Not any more. Things are moving faster now. The poison is affecting you faster, and it will take effect the moment you leave this world to return to your own.' She looked at Evan. 'I can see it in her eyes. She has an hour at most and then she needs human air to breath, if she is to clear the poison from her system. Do you understand?'

'Yes,' said Evan.

'Same as us,' growled Arn. 'This world is killing me and Aurora, too. The strain of getting here was too much. We must flee as well.'

Evan looked at Nell. 'We can't do it. There isn't time.'

'Yes there is,' said Loki. 'Lammergeyer.'

He looked up, cupped his hand round his mouth and gave a loud whistle. Then he shouted, 'Eanmor.'

Laki squeezed her arm. 'You're going to love this. Eanmor is the best. I know you hate Loki and he plays around with people all the time, but he loves Eanmor. He trained her only with kindness.'

A moment later a dark dot appeared in the sky over the ice palace and grew rapidly as it soared towards them and became one of the huge hang-glider-sized birds. As it soared over their heads, the down-draught from its wings buffeted them, and Nell held on to Evan as he staggered, his body still thawing and weak.

It circled a couple of times and then Loki whistled it again, and it stalled and began to descend right above them, growing in size. They had to duck and hold on to their hoods with their hands, like people shielding themselves from a helicopter's blades.

Nell winced as she saw its claws hit the ground. She'd still got the marks from the last time she was taken up by one of these birds. But then she spotted the leather harness over its bronze feathers and a simple sling below.

The bird turned a fearsome beak towards Loki, who ran over and stroked its great feathery head. The hot metal smell enveloped them.

'She's mine. I raised her from a chick. So take care of her.'

'Quickly,' said Laki. 'Lammergeyers don't wait around. If they stay on the ground too long they find it difficult to take off again.'

Good. That gave Nell no chance to worry about the flimsiness of the sling, or the fact that it was meant to carry one but she and Evan were cramming into it and holding each other with one hand and holding the leather strapping with the other.

No sooner had they got the straps around them than Loki gave Eanmor a final pat and they were rising into the air, higher and higher. There was no use screaming, or trying to ask Evan if this was safe. There was only one sound. The *whump* of the wings going down, a pause, then the *whump* again, and a pause, until they were high above the ice.

Nell opened her eyes without realizing she'd closed

them, and saw the Mother Harp in the distance, touching the clouds. The air burned like ice up here. She looked down. Loki, Laki and the Vanir were dots on the black lake.

Eanmor stopped rising, angled her great wings and, after a moment when nothing happened, started flying towards the harp.

It took a few minutes, that was all. Even so Nell thought she was going to fall off with the cold. Even the goose feathers couldn't keep out this degree of cold. It was the temperature that you'd find at the centre of the universe. Ancient cold that had never seen any heat ever. It was too frozen to fill her lungs.

I'll just fall off and die if we don't get there soon, she thought. Evan was OK, he was half Ice Elven now. He held her and tried to warm her. Then he undid his jacket and pulled her close and wrapped it round them both.

'Hold on,' he said. 'We're nearly there.'

The Mother Harp rose and rose and Nell felt her hair begin to stand on end. Goose bumps ran up and down her arms. She felt her teeth start to tingle and her eyes ache when she looked at it. It was just one huge needle of power, rising so high she couldn't see the top in the darkening sky.

The harp strings radiating out from it came down a mile away from it. Great black lines etched on the air and plummeting down from the darkness above.

She wasn't the only one feeling its effects. Eanmor began to slow. They could feel the reluctance in her wings. She was putting on the brakes.

Evan shouted something in Elven to her. The bird screeched and tried to turn, but Evan shouted out again, and this time she gave a long, painful cry but carried on flying towards the harp.

'I have to make her go on,' said Evan. 'She wants to turn. Loki told me to give her that order. It's a command she won't disobey.'

Poor Eanmor, thought Nell, as the bird fought the waves of power coming from the harp. She can feel that the harp might kill her. Like it had killed the little birds round the other harps.

'We're making her fly, when she's scared stiff,' said Nell. 'She knows she's in danger.'

Evan squeezed her hand. 'Worry later. Come on.'

They were so close, now. The huge harp was filling their view. It was wider than anything she'd seen before.

Eanmor stalled again. Evan shouted the command.

She doesn't know why we're making her do this, thought Nell, sadly. She doesn't know we're trying to save the world. She's just trying to save herself.

A moment later the lammergeyer gave another cry, unlike the others. It was a final, sad caw, and her great wings faltered.

Nell clung to the harness, her ears popping as they dropped.

This was why Eanmor had been trying to turn round. She could feel herself dying.

As the lammergeyer began to flutter weakly towards the ground, circling lower and lower like a sycamore seed, Nell knew they'd forced her to her death.

But they'd made it.

Seventeen

And so it was that Elven and human,
In deep midwinter, by frosty moonlight,
Went hand in hand over the killer ice,
To play the new world into being.

As Nell brushed the snow off her jacket and stood up unsteadily, the saga verse ran on a loop through her mind. She stamped her feet, trying to get her blood flowing again. Compared to the sky, it was almost warm down here. If warm was twenty below zero. But at least there was no killer wind. They'd entered the eye of the storm again, and around them everything was eerily still.

Must get moving. Must play the world into being again. She crossed her fingers and silently prayed, *Please, let it work.*

Behind her Eanmor was a huge heap of bronze feathers

265

and leather harness – totally still apart from her wing flapping upwards as Evan crawled out and staggered to his feet.

We killed her. So please let it work. Please don't let it be for nothing.

'Come on,' said Evan. 'Nearly there.'

They started walking. They were so close to the harp she could hardly bear to look at it. It was truly frightening. It was too big, too solid, too powerful. In scale, they were like two ants walking towards a stone pillar. Her focus went in and out as she tried to work out whether it was near or still far away. Their hair stood on end as though they were near static. No wonder Eanmor had fallen. Her fingertips sparked angrily, her teeth tingled.

Above, in the lurid sky, there was a whirlpool of cloud spinning and twisting in on itself as though it was being tortured and wanted to be free of the giant needle that was pinning it there.

A few more hours and it will be free, thought Nell, free of the human world altogether, like a balloon with a broken string.

'If it stops now – what will happen to us?'

'We'll go spinning off into space and time,' said Evan. 'We'll be stranded on an ice world in an icy void. All alone on a dark lake. And Krake will get his way and start building another world, and you'll be the only warm being on it, and in the end your heart will almost stop and your blood will freeze and we'll become like them.'

He was trying to sound calm but she could hear the panic in his voice. She knew why. The nearer they got, the more the harp seemed to be pushing them away. No wind blew, but it was as though they were the same poles of a magnet being pushed apart by an invisible force. It didn't want them near, that was for sure. She became convinced it would like to throw them back, stop their hearts completely and squidge them into atoms.

'What's it made of?' she gasped as they toiled closer, hanging on to each other's hands.

'Raw magic,' said Evan. 'That's what we know from the writings of the Vanir. It's the same thing that the rest of the universe is made of. But more condensed. More dangerous.'

'Raw magic?' Nell gave a laugh. 'I love it. But Mr Siddons, our Science teacher, wouldn't agree. He says that the universe is made up of matter and dark matter and dark energy.'

'It's just different words, Nell. I bet they mean the same thing. Magic, dark matter, what's the difference?'

Nell leaned back and looked up. The towering black column seemed to rise up into the air and go on for ever, disappearing into the whirlwind of clouds.

'How tall is it?'

'According to the sagas, it links through time and space and keeps our world and your world tethered together.'

'Pretty big, then.'

She'd thought it was black, but as they got nearer, she could see two dwarfed and tiny figures approaching opposite them. It was their reflections. The harp was a dark mirror. But it reflected nothing else, not the sky nor the lake behind them, nor Eanmor. Nell shivered. It was as though it was alive and thinking, and had decided to focus solely on them.

'Does it know we've come to help, do you think?' whispered Nell.

'Hope so.'

And as they got nearer, she saw that it wasn't just a dark mirror, but that there was a subtle patterning on it. Something was visible beneath the surface, an inner structure, like a double spiral.

'I've seen that spiral before,' said Nell. 'It's the double helix. We both have DNA, that's what we're made of.'

'Maybe it's a mixture of human and Elven. That's why it takes both of us.'

A few more steps, no more than crossing a road, and they would be right beside it. They would touch it. Nell could see herself clearly in its dark glass now.

'I look different,' she said.

Evan gave a laugh. 'I wondered when you'd notice. It's been happening for a while. Ever since you used Elven charm.'

Her hair was lighter than its usual dark brown. In the weird light it looked as though she'd had expensive three-coloured highlights. And her eyes – were they going darker, like charcoal?

They covered the last few metres and then they were there, right in front of it, within touching distance. A faint hum was emanating from it. And a smell of ozone, like at the seaside, or when her mum brought the washing in from outside. They stood together, opposite their reflections. She looked at herself and then at Evan beside her. His hair had gone darker, his eyes lighter.

'We're going to end up equal,' she said.

He grinned. 'Two freaks. Me half Ice Elven. You half Elven.'

She regarded her mirror-image. 'I am becoming Elven, aren't I? I can charm. I think I always had that skill, just a little. If I didn't want to be noticed I could sort of fade out of everyone's thoughts. Then since you left, I've noticed it more. And once in Drama, when I didn't want to get chosen, I heard bees buzzing and I realized it was me, and no one was taking any notice of me, as if I wasn't there.'

He felt his pulse. 'And my heart has slowed right down till it's almost stopped. A beat a month, that's all it'll do from now onwards.'

Their eyes met in their reflection. 'Cool. My friend – the undead boy – and me,' said Nell. 'Saving a world. Doesn't seem likely.'

'If not us – who else?' he said. 'We're unique.'

A thought struck her. 'Let's hope we can still activate the harp.'

She reached a tentative hand towards its slick hard surface, and then drew her hand back. She daren't touch it. Maybe her fingers would instantly freeze and fall off as though dipped in liquid nitrogen. She told herself not to be so stupid. It was called the *Mother* Harp. It hadn't been called the Demon Harp or the Killer Harp or the Mad Psycho Harp. The name Mother had to count for something.

So she reached out again, and this time when she touched it, it rippled in an odd way. Not like liquid, or molten plastic. More like a thick gas.

'What do we do?' she said.

'Aurora said we've got to read the words on it.'

'I don't see any.'

They began to search along the harp's surface.

'It could be anywhere,' said Nell, desperately.

'No, it's here,' said Evan.

He was right, words were forming on the dark surface. The harp had stopped trying to push them away. Maybe that had been the Vanir's equivalent of a burglar alarm. Now they were next to it, it seemed to be helping.

'It's in old Elven runes,' he said. 'I can just about make it out.'

'But it's only words,' said Nell, staring blankly at them. 'How can words start anything up?'

He caught her hand and held it tight. 'Because words are sounds, and sound has power. In the beginning was the word.'

Nell nodded and squeezed his hand. 'OK. You tell me what to say, and then we'll repeat it together.'

He began murmuring the ancient words, and Nell listened and copied. At first their voices sounded tiny and pitiful against the bulk of the harp and the expanse of ice behind them. But then they became stronger and seemed to echo and fill the air.

When the last rune had been spoken, they stopped and waited, patiently.

Nothing happened, but somehow she'd stopped worrying. Nell the worrier had become calm. It seemed stupid to get all panicky because if the worse was

271

going to happen there wasn't anything they could do to stop it.

They waited. And waited. And waited some more. Still nothing happened. She turned to Evan and looped her arms round his neck. 'I think we might have to kiss. Aurora started them playing with her human boyfriend. I bet they didn't just hold hands.'

Suddenly he looked just like the boys at school, impish and foxy. He put his arms tight round her neck. 'Or maybe we have to do something more?'

She laughed. 'You wish.'

Their faces were inches apart. Little sparks of static were flashing and clicking between them.

'I want to kiss you anyway, just in case,' he said.

So he did, right there beneath the harp in the weird purple light, with their hair standing out like a dandelion's. Her first true kiss. Strange. Soft. Sweet. And pretty painful because of the sparks that flew between their lips and zapped off their teeth.

And the next moment they were hugging and kissing and almost falling over, until they bumped up against the harp. And this time it didn't ripple beneath them, it gave way.

As they tried to get their balance, they sank through the blackness, through the mirror surface, through the shadows of the double helix, into somewhere else. They stumbled and almost fell to their knees, but holding on to each other, they regained their balance.

They were in pitch blackness. Not just dark, but the total absence of light. They wrapped their arms round each other.

'Don't let go this time,' she whispered.

His voice came out of the void. 'Never.'

She took a deep breath. 'Hello?' she called uncertainly. 'Anyone there? Um. Hello. We need you to start up again.'

The silence stretched. Nell began to feel that they weren't inside the harp but floating in the blackness of space, with no up or down, no left or right. She couldn't feel the ground beneath her feet any more.

'Can you talk to a giant device?' said Evan.

'It's called Mother. So maybe.' She had the feeling that there wasn't just silence around them, but the silence you get when someone is keeping very still and listening. Maybe if you made such a huge powerful device and gave it a name, it also got a personality.

So she tried again, louder this time.

'Can you restart the harps, please? We don't want to go spinning off into space. Elven and humans should be close together, not in separate dimensions or whatever.'

Somewhere close but far away, something seemed to say *ha!* Or maybe it was the echo of their breathing.

'It's true,' she said firmly. 'And maybe it's time for them to come out of the mist, to stop hiding and to join our world openly.'

There was a sound that could've been a quiet laugh. Not a nasty one. But someone being mildly amused by her. Or it might only have been a breeze blowing through the nothingness around them.

'No. I'm serious. It could happen. It takes both sides to want it, though. It's not just the humans' fault that the two ended up enemies. The Elven have to want to make friends as well!'

Evan was staring at her. How – when it was totally dark? She looked around. Because it wasn't as dark now, or she was seeing with something other than her eyes.

'The Elven come out of the mist?' he said, taken aback. 'What – and show the world we're real?'

Nell laughed. 'Just imagine!'

'Chaos.'

They both started laughing and hugging each other as though they'd never let go. Whatever the differences between Elven and human, whatever the wars and misunderstandings that had been going on for a thousand years, they didn't exist for Nell and Evan.

'Perfect harmony,' she whispered. 'Maybe this time it will work out better.'

And then they seemed to get tangled up in the double helix and all they could see were spiralling lines, moving and turning now.

A big sigh went over them that seemed to say *yes* at the same time. Or it could've been the great structure flexing. But in any case, the harp began to hum, like a tuning fork. That stopped them laughing. They looked around. They were back outside the harp again. They let go of each other and clapped their hands over their ears. Nell fell to her knees, suddenly dizzy and weak and unable to balance. For a moment her head whirled and then she managed to look up. Evan was staring down at her.

'Is it working?' she cried, over the increasing hum. 'Is it restarting?'

Still he stared. His face had become stricken again.

'Never mind that,' he said. 'We've got to get you out of here.'

What was he seeing in her eyes? The poison of the Elven world that would turn toxic the moment she returned through the mist? What good would restarting the world be, if she could never return to her own world for fear of becoming old in an instant?

'How long have I been here?'

'Too long,' he said.

Eighteen

The humming got louder and more insistent.

Evan pulled Nell up and they ran – back towards the great heap of feathers that had been Eanmor the lammergeyer. Every part of her felt weak. All she wanted to do was collapse on to the ice. But she could feel that hum building, feel the static on the back of her neck. It wound up the scale, going higher and higher. She heard Evan curse and cry out in pain, as it rose towards the kind of pitch that only dogs can hear.

Then it peaked and hovered on one note, but they kept running. The one note, high and painful, sang out above them. And stopped. A terrible silence held.

Nell and Evan both looked back. The Mother Harp was sitting there, blocking the view, too solid, too real. Nell cringed, as though she was waiting for a loud firework to go off. If the harp exploded then that would be the end of both of them.

'Why's it stopped?' she said.

It went *BOOM*. But silently.

A surge of power rippled out at hyper-speed, like a stone thrown into a pond, sending circles of power coursing across the black ice. They ducked and held on to their heads as it sizzled overhead. It was like being hit by the biggest bass drum beat ever, combined with the squeal of a note so high up the scale she could hardly hear it. It thudded through her chest, tickled her eardrums, shook her ribs, vibrated her eyes, slid her along the ice until the bulk of Eanmor stopped her. By her side, Evan slid with her and groaned and clutched his hair and curled into a ball. Until suddenly it had passed over and moved on. A ringing silence fell.

Nell uncurled and crawled slowly around Eanmor's body and got a view of the lake. Within seconds she saw the ripple hit the harp where she'd nearly drowned. Ice and frost streamed off its highest point like gigantic banners. The strings holding it up became a blur. Were they vibrating again?

'Please let them be starting to sing,' said Evan, reading her mind.

She got to her knees, using Eanmor's bronze feathers as handholds. Then Evan pulled her to her feet. They watched together as the ripple swept on, hitting the edge of the Elven forest, blasting the frozen trees, sending huge clouds of atomized snow into the air as it powered past, travelling on and out towards the great circle of the lesser harps.

'Nothing can stop it, surely?' said Nell.

'No.'

They held their breaths and listened. At first all they could hear was the bass thunder as it swept along, spreading out and out, followed by the tickling, high-pitched drone that accompanied it. But wait – what was that? They both angled their heads towards the forest. Softly and hesitant, like a tiny child first learning to sing 'Twinkle, Twinkle, Little Star', the harps were beginning to play again. A trickle of notes getting faster and developing a melody.

'It worked,' said Evan flatly, as though he hardly dare believe it.

'It did,' said Nell, just as calmly. 'We did it.' A bubble of laughter rose up in her, even though her stomach had begun churning and she thought she might be sick. 'We blimmin' did it.'

He gave a wild laugh. He leaped into the air. '*It worked!*'

He grabbed her and swung her round, laughing. But then he stopped laughing. He'd remembered. She could see it wash over his face. He'd remembered as soon as he looked at her. Did she looked different? Were the poisons showing on her face?

'It's impossible, isn't it?' she said. 'I can't get back in time now.'

He shook his head. 'We'll flit.'

Yes, but only when they reached the edge of the ice and the start of the forest. It would take them hours to do that.

'We've only got minutes, haven't we?' Images of home and her mum on the sofa watching TV flashed through her mind. Of going into town with Gwen, buying clothes, learning to play the drums.

She turned to Evan. 'Do something. I can't think straight at the moment.'

'Let me think,' he said, desperately.

She sank to her knees. She was too worn out to move or think.

'Wait, what's that?' he said.

Three dots in the sky were coming towards them at great speed. She stopped on her knees, with Evan by her side. The dots grew wings, became birds, became much bigger birds.

'Lammergeyers,' she said.

Now they could see Loki and Laki beneath two of

them, swinging their legs down, coming in to land beneath the giant birds. And one free one, following the others and coming to a wing-beating, flapping, down-draught stop above them, then landing as lightly as a sparrow on a lawn.

'You did it,' said Laki. 'You're really amazing.'

Nell swallowed something bitter. 'Yeah, you'll have plenty of time to remind me – when I'm stuck here.'

Laki hugged her. 'Silly. You'll be fine. Although I'd quite like you staying here for ever.'

Nell stared at her. Laki took her shoulders and shook her. 'The lammergeyers, dummy. They'll fly you to the forest in a minute. They'll fly you home in fifteen.'

Evan had understood already. He ran to the huge birds and began adjusting the harnesses, his face cleared of dread.

'Come on,' he shouted. 'Let's get you home.'

'Wait.'

She didn't want to do this, but she had to. She walked over to Loki. He was standing by his fallen bird's head, which was stretched out along the ice, the neck limp and twisted. A few smaller feathers, that were still as long as a peacock's tail feather, were strewn on the ice. Loki picked one up and stroked it against his face.

'Sorry,' she said. What else could she say?

He gave her his usual mocking glance, but she could see he was upset.

'She wanted to turn round, but we made her carry on flying to the Mother Harp. She obeyed and then she fell from the sky.'

'I know. I saw her,' said Loki. 'She's a brave bird.'

Was a brave bird, thought Nell sadly, until the bronze feathers suddenly shook and a tremor ran through the long neck.

Eanmor raised her head. Her beak, as long and hooked as a pirate's cutlass, swung round in a drunken circle. Nell and Loki ducked.

'Oh. She's alive!'

Loki went closer and looked into the stunned bird's eye. 'Only just.'

Nell gave a relieved laugh. 'I thought we'd killed her. I hated the thought, even though we'd saved the world.'

Loki had a hand on the bird's deadly beak, as though Eanmor was a dog he was checking over. 'Go,' he said. 'You don't want to be old.' He glanced at her. 'Then I wouldn't be able to argue with you.'

Nell hesitated. 'What made you help us?'

He stroked Eanmor's feathers and didn't look at her as he said, 'We came to your world to stop you and Evan. We were Ice Elven, we despised humans – even though

282

we'd never met any. Then we ran into you, Nell.' He stopped stroking and turned to her. She could see it was hard for him to say this. 'I never imagined a human would be so brave, and actually fight their way over the ice.'

Nell shivered. 'And under it.'

'And tell our god he was wrong.' He grinned at her. It was still mocking and dangerous, but there was something else there as well. 'You're brave. Ice Elven admire that. We salute it.'

He gave her a mocking salute.

She nodded in thanks, keeping it modest. But inside she was thinking, yes, it *was* amazing. Me and Evan saving a world. And getting an Ice Elven to admit we were right. 'Thanks for helping us in the end.'

Loki glanced over at Evan, who was impatiently waiting with a lammergeyer rein in each hand. 'I'll probably regret it.'

'Don't,' she said. 'Just because you're Ice Elven, it doesn't mean you have to cut yourselves off and hate everyone else. Chill out.'

Loki held out one of Eanmor's feathers to her. 'Take it and remember us.' His face went sly and wicked again. 'We'll come and visit your world again. We'll run rings around you.'

'You could try.' She tucked the feather into the jacket

of her goose suit. 'I'll keep scraps for Eanmor. As a treat.'

Then she turned and tried to run back to Evan, but her legs were too weak. Laki ran and looped an arm around her neck and dragged her to Evan, who helped her into the harness and did the straps up.

'Ice Elven,' he muttered. 'Always thinking they're the best.'

Nell laughed. 'Prove you're the best. Get me back home.'

He ran to his bird.

'Hug.' Laki held out her arms and hugged her. 'I got a human friend. Amazing.'

'Come and visit,' said Nell. 'Come for tea.'

If she hadn't been feeling so ill she would have laughed to herself, thinking of her mum getting the tea ready, and them sitting round the TV, or in front of the computer, eating pizza slices from plates on their knees.

The bird lurched and flapped, sending ice and snow flying. Nell felt her stomach drop and then steady itself and then drop again as the bird flapped upwards with its powerful wings – *whump*, pause, *whump*, pause, *whump*, pause – and then it hung in the air again for a moment, above Loki and Laki and their lammergeyers. It stretched its neck, the metallic feathers glinting in the purple light, and began to fly at speed towards the forest.

The cold hit her again, and before her eyes began to mist over with freezing tears she saw Evan soaring beside her and leading her lammergeyer towards the trees.

She looked down and saw the spires and towers of the Ice Elven palace, and the grey circle around the nearby harp where she'd risen from the ice, as though being born again. The edge of the forest was closing fast. And beyond it were the other harps, spaced out across the forest, marching right to the horizon. In the distance she could see the bursts of snow and ice as the sound wave of the Mother Harp continued its journey outwards, waking every harp it passed over. She pushed her hood back slightly and listened. The melody was strong enough to reach them up here now.

They'd done it. She closed her eyes. She could relax now. They were on the way home.

'Nell?'

She opened her eyes and glanced over at Evan. He was flying beside her, looking at her anxiously. She tried to give him a wave, to show him she was all right, but her hand had frozen on to the harness and wouldn't let go.

Had she fallen asleep? Had she been dreaming? She shook herself and looked down. They were flying over the palace of the Rivers great-family. The harp nearest to it, the one she'd walked through when she first came to the forest, was starting to sing again. Soon Star would be able to take all the little ones back to their home. Soon Lettie wouldn't be on her own and the children could eat sugary human cereals for breakfast and rot their teeth, and argue with each other, and get Evan to sort it all out.

Her eyes closed.

'Nell. Wake up. We're nearly there.'

But she couldn't make her eyes open. Maybe they were iced closed. She really was too tired to care. But the lammergeyer thought otherwise. It suddenly stalled, throwing her forwards, and then dropping rapidly so her stomach got left behind.

This time she managed to half open her eyes and peer downwards in a daze.

Below was a clearing with clumps of mist showing through the trees. She was nearly home. Nearly. It was getting closer and closer. Then the ground was right there, and Evan was unstrapping her harness and she felt herself being picked up. He was running with her in his arms and the mist was closing in on her face, cold and clammy but getting thinner.

She smelled the car exhaust smell of her own world. And other arms were reaching for her now. She heard her dad's voice. And Nan's.

'She's got the poisoning. She only just made it back.'
Evan's voice.

And Dad was carrying her fast through the trees, twigs
catching in her hair. Then they were both shouting orders.

'Open the car door.'

'That's it, lay her on my knee.' That was Nan. 'Not to
the hospital. She needs specialist care.'

'You sure?'

'Positive. She needs a detox.'

'My place, then.'

The car door slammed. The engine fired into life.

'Wait for Evan,' she said, but they didn't listen to her.

Her last thought, before a buzzing blackness engulfed
her, was this:

She'd made it. She'd crossed the ice, she'd survived the
Ice Elven palace, she'd almost drowned, she'd argued
with a god. But she and Evan had done it. Together they'd
started the harps, and saved the world.

Nineteen

Nell didn't know how long she slept, tossing and turning, hot and feverish. She could hear snow falling, hissing softly at the windows near where she lay, tucked up and safe under a quilt.

Sometimes the wind blew, and it was as though pebbles were being thrown at the window. Then she would go to sleep again, still aching and burning up. But at last she woke up properly.

She lay still, without the energy to call out and say she was awake. She tried to sit up, but it was as though the air had turned into a thin membrane that she was too weak to fight through. So she lay back and looked around. In front of her there was a row of windows, reflecting the yellow lights of the street. A digital clock said 12.30.

She sniffed the air. Coffee and toast. She raised her head. She must have made some kind of noise because she heard footsteps. A hand stroked her brow.

'Lie back, relax.' Her dad?

'Wha' happened?' she said, trying to sit up again.

The hands pushed her back down. 'You stayed a long time in the Elven world. You nearly got poisoned. Drink this.'

A cup touched her lips and then a bitter liquid withered her mouth and burned her throat.

The thick buzzing blackness started to erode her vision again, and she sank back and gave way to it. Some time later she woke to see a watery dawn coming in through the windows. She rolled over and looked out. It was a street she recognized. This was where her dad lived. She was in his house. Lying on his sofa.

'Good, you're awake. Drink this.'

She tried to push the cup away, but this time her nan held her head firmly and pushed the cup between her dry lips. She choked and spat, but the hands held her firm.

'It's Chinese herbs, that's all. They taste bad, but they'll get rid of the poison.'

In the end she drank and then lay down again, her head cradled on Dru's lap, and Dru's hands stroking her forehead again. After a while the hands pulled a quilt up high around her neck, tucking it in, making her secure, then smoothing her damp forehead. This time she slept less feverishly.

When she woke she could hear people talking. Her dad and Dru. They were still trying to poison her. She could smell the horrible bitter drink as it was put close to her mouth.

'Drink up, Nell. It'll do you good.'

Then a more impatient voice. 'Duh! Just hold her nose and pour it down her throat, for heaven's sake.'

So Gwen was there as well, sounding bored. No, not bored, even though she wasn't getting all the attention as usual. Nell opened her eyes a little and squinted around. It was like one of those death-bed scenes in old novels. Her nan and her dad sitting round her, looking anxious. Although Gwen spoiled it by sitting on the arm of the sofa and impatiently tapping her beautiful nails on the wall behind.

When she saw Nell open her eyes a little, she leaned closer and said, 'Get your act together, I've got to *talk* to you. Now. Soon.'

'Leave her,' said Dad. 'She's been ill. Let her rest.'

Gwen said, 'Hmmm,' and disappeared from view.

At first she couldn't think why she was here, then everything flooded back.

'We did it,' she said. She laughed but that hurt so she

stopped. 'We started the harps.'

Dru nodded. 'Yes. Working perfectly, apparently.'

Nell managed to sit up. 'How long have I been ill?'

'You got back yesterday evening. It's now midday. A night and a day.'

She looked at Dru and her dad. 'Does Mum know?'

'She was here all last night. She thinks you've had food poisoning, from the sledging party. We said you ate sausages that hadn't been cooked properly. We said lots of others had come down with it.'

'What about Gwen?'

Dad and Dru glanced at each other. 'She thinks food poisoning as well.'

Suddenly the memory of that last wild ride back to this world came back to her. 'Where's Evan?'

'Back in the forest, where he belongs.' Her dad's hands went into fists and he cracked his knuckles as though he was wishing they were Evan's bones. Didn't he realize that he'd got her back here safely?

'Why are you so angry with him?' She kicked the quilt off and swung her legs round, so she was sitting on the sofa properly.

'He nearly got you killed,' said Tom in his sternest police voice. 'I told him never to come back round here. I made a deal – if he promised never to see you again, we'd leave him alone. He agreed. Apparently the Elven are hot on keeping their word.'

'Oh, OK.'

She pretended to be disappointed, but really she was thinking – we'll see about that. The Elven had a way of promising things so cleverly that they outsmarted everyone. But there was something much more important that she wanted confirmed.

'So you'll be opening the iron camps now,' she said, looking at Dru.

Straight away she knew that this wasn't the case. Her grandmother looked away.

'I wish, Nell. I really do. I've been in touch with Stan Larson. Remember him? The twerp who used to be my immediate boss. I said exactly the same thing to him. The Elven world is no longer dying. So if we release the Elven in the camps, they would go back to their own home.'

'How could he argue with that?' said Nell, leaning forward eagerly. 'They've got no reason to move here permanently any more.'

Dru made an angry noise. 'Doesn't make any difference. Stan Larson and the other leaders won't budge. They say now that the Ice Elven have shown their faces here, it's too dangerous.'

Nell couldn't believe what she was hearing. 'But the Ice

Elven never wanted to come here in the first place. They like their icy lake.' She shivered, remembering being underneath it, with Krake spiralling up from its depths. 'They won't be a threat.'

'Stan says that until we have a way of stopping the Elven – Ice and Forest – from entering our world when they want, they'll have to keep the Elven in the camps.'

'That's stupid!' Nell tried to jump to her feet, but all that happened was her head swam and she had to sit down again. She lay back and closed her eyes and took a few deep breaths.

We'll see about that as well, she thought, furiously.

She spent the afternoon plotting and planning.

By the evening she felt well enough to get up and have a shower. She stared for a long time at her hair in the bathroom mirror. It was fairer, and had light streaks in it.

I like it, she thought. It's my hidden, recessive Elven genes coming out. Somewhere in the Church family tree, there must have been an Elven ancestor. Maybe some girl way back had fallen for a white-haired boy she met in the forest, and later had a baby. And ever after, down through the generations, little traces of the Elven genes had been passed on. For Dru and her dad it had meant they were immune to the Elven charm. But she'd managed to awaken more of those hidden genes in herself.

She was able to charm.

I'm becoming half and half. If anyone can save the Elven, it should be me.

She had a plan. It was pretty extreme, but it could work. No, it *had* to work, and quickly. Soon it would be Evan's little sister's birthday. When she'd first seen Evan, on the night of the snow party, he'd said it was in two weeks. Three days later they'd entered the forest and made their way to the ice. A day later she was back, and she'd been lying here in her dad's house for a day. That meant there was just over a week to go before Duck's birthday.

Wouldn't it be brilliant if I could get them all released in time for that?

She stared at herself some more. She was remembering being inside that great Mother Harp with Evan. They'd talked about how the future could be for Elven and human. They'd laughed back then, but now she wasn't laughing.

She finished getting ready, then tottered downstairs on legs that were still shaky. And found something strange. Her mum had arrived to check on her. She was sitting on a stool by the breakfast bar talking to Dad. Sitting in the same room, in his house, talking and discussing things without shouting. Amazing. Almost as amazing as her plan.

If those two can stop arguing then my idea just might work.

Next day, when Dru offered her another evil Chinese brew for breakfast, she got straight up and said she was going home. Dru argued, saying maybe there were still some Elven poisons in her body, and she wasn't strong enough yet. Luckily Gwen came by at that moment, in full Queen Bee mode, and declared that Nell looked a mess but well again. She told her grandmother that Nell needed fresh air instead of lying around being waited on hand and foot, and then dragged her out of the house.

The wind was still bitter but Nell didn't feel it. She was wrapped in the goose suit again. Gwen had given it a thoughtful and surprised inspection and approved.

'If you could get hold of some more of those, I could start a fashion line,' she said, as they walked quickly through the frozen streets.

Maybe, but none of them would have Eanmor's beautiful bronze feather tucked inside, like Nell's. She'd found Loki's parting gift to her when she'd put the jacket on, and decided to keep it there. It still gave off a slight hot metallic smell that reminded her instantly of the big bird that had nearly given her life to help them, and sometimes reminded her of Loki's wicked face, looking at her with something like respect for a few moments. If she could get someone like him on her side, then she could do anything.

'Where are we going?' Nell asked after a while.

But Gwen said nothing. They seemed to be heading towards the school. It was still closed for the Christmas holiday, extended because of the snow and a broken boiler. So much had happened in the few weeks since the end of term. She'd found Evan again, so now she didn't have to daydream about him any more. They'd shared their first proper kiss – inside a huge, nearly magical harp, for heaven's sake! She gave a laugh and Gwen glanced at her, but said nothing.

'Come on, this way.'

Gwen led her through a gap in the school fence and on to the playing fields. They began tramping over the thick frozen snow covering the football pitches, over the hockey pitches, to the far forgotten corner where the old sports pavilion sat. The snow around it was trampled by footprints. The windows were still shuttered to keep anyone from seeing inside.

Gwen stopped at the door. 'You wait. You'll see how busy I've been whilst you were lying there throwing up, and groaning and getting everyone running round after you.' She tapped out a rhythm on the door.

'I was ill. I had food poisoning.'

'Yeah, of course you did.' Gwen gave her a strange look. 'You're not the only one who can remember the Elven now. I can.'

A cloud of warmth billowed out at them as the door swung open.

She didn't move. She stared at her sister. 'So your Elven genes have woken up too!'

'I have no idea what you're talking about,' said Gwen. She gave Nell a push. 'In you go, superstar.'

Inside, waiting for her, were the Elven. Nell took in the scene in one swift glance. There was Falcon with his hand still on the door. Star over by the stove, which was blasting out heat. Fen, huddled in a corner on a sagging old sofa, looking like a rock star who needed rehab. But her gaze stopped on Evan. He'd looked up from a laptop they'd rigged up in the corner. The pavilion now had electricity, too. He must have been busy stealing power from the nearest cables. He stood up but he didn't move when he saw her. He stayed as still as a statue. He looked scared to death.

That wasn't the case with Star. She gave a squeal and ran up to Nell, her plaits flying, and hugged her. When she finally let go she stood back and looked Nell up and down and stared into her eyes.

'Hmmm. The poison has nearly gone,' she said. 'But you should have let me nurse you. I'm the best.'

Nell grinned. 'I wish you had, but I didn't get a choice. It was the worst experience ever. My nan nearly poisoned me with these horrible bitter herbs.'

Star looked surprised, and a bit disappointed. 'Oh, no that's right. Your grandmama knew what she was doing. That's how I would've done it, too.'

'But what are you all doing here?'

Falcon came over. 'Using it as a base, until the rest of us are free.'

He grinned at her, then thumped her arm, lightly, as though she was a boy Elven. 'Starting the harps – that's not bad for a human . . .' He paused. Nell waited. 'But I could've done the same I'm sure.'

Nell nodded in agreement, which made him look surprised. 'Yeah, you could. But there had to be the boy-girl bit. That's all.' She was being kind to him, she could see how much he'd wanted to save the world. 'Doesn't matter whether it was two Elven or one Elven and one human. It's all the same.'

Now it was Evan's turn. She had to walk over to him. He was still frozen.

'Hey,' he managed, when she was standing in front of him.

'Don't worry. I know Dad made you promise.' She walked a step closer and smiled. 'See? It's me approaching you, not you getting in contact with me. You didn't break your word.' She laughed. 'I'm as tricky as an Elven.'

Evan shook his head. 'It's not that.' He bit his lip. 'I thought I'd killed you.' He inspected her as closely as Star had done. 'Are you sure you're OK?'

She held out her arms. 'See, I'm fine. I'm still alive. I'm hard to kill.'

He let out a sigh of relief and then he hugged her – right in front of all the others. And she wrapped her own arms tight around him. She heard Fen give a sharp intake of breath. She heard her sister give a chuckle and then say, 'Well, hey, whaddayaknow. Go, Nell.'

She didn't care. She didn't care what any of them thought. When they finally let go of each other, Evan said, 'Did your grandmother manage to talk to the Watchers? Are they opening the camps?'

She shook her head, and saw his face drop. 'I'm working on it,' she said. 'Trust me.'

He nodded. Then he took her hand and held it up. 'We did it. We started the harps. Elven and human. Nell is now an honorary Elven.'

Fen made a noise. Nell swung round. His face was sour. But that wasn't a surprise to her. The surprise was that her sister, who'd suffered at his hands, was sitting next to him.

Nell let go of Evan and went over.

'You do remember everything, right?' she said to Gwen. 'You remember what he did to you?'

Gwen looked pleased with herself. 'Yep. Everything.'

Fen narrowed his eyes and gave a snarl.

Gwen leaned closer and nudged him sharply with her elbow. 'Shut up,' she said.

He winced and glared at her. 'You dare to—'

'Yes, I do,' said Gwen, in her ice-queen voice. 'I dare to tell you to shut up and stop snarling at my sister. It's rude. You really want me to explain again how you're not going to bully humans any more?'

Fen tried to outstare her, but that was never going to work, not with Gwen in this sort of mood. In the end he leaned back and muttered, 'No. Leave me, I'm ill. I need rest.'

Gwen folded her arms. 'You'll get rest. But when you wake up I will always be here to remind you not to take

301

advantage of human girls ever again.'

Fen's face was a picture. Nell wanted to laugh. He'd met his match with Gwen.

'When did you start remembering?' she asked.

Gwen shrugged. 'After we got back from the woods. But I thought I was going crazy. I kept seeing his face. Then when you went back through the mist with Evan, and I heard Nan and Dad panicking, it all came back to me.' She stood up and moved away, pulling Nell with her. 'I went to the woods. I found the mist. I stood there and yelled until someone came.'

'She wouldn't shut up,' said Falcon. He'd followed them, and was giving Gwen the sort of doting look that Nell knew well.

'Ah.' Gwen patted his cheek. 'He's cute. I like Falcon.'

Falcon's face turned a light shade of pink, like the most delicate rose. He was blushing.

'The last time Becca thought an Elven was cute, she ended up under his spell,' said Nell.

She'd been worrying about that. Loki might have saved her life by loaning her the lammergeyer, and she might be keeping the feather tucked in her jacket – but that didn't help Becca. He'd screwed up her mind with his Ice Elven powers.

'Oh, he came back yesterday,' said Gwen. 'He put it all right. He made Becca forget everything that had happened. He says he's sorry. I don't altogether believe him. He's cute but bad.' She looked back at Fen. 'Almost as bad as big brother there. But I'll make sure he doesn't do any more harm. I've got to face my fears.'

Nell looked at her sister with admiration. She was right. You couldn't run away from things that scared you. They had to be faced. Gwen was facing Fen, so she had to as well.

She went back over to him and sat on the arm of the sofa. She remembered his face looming over hers as he'd hexed her. She remembered him spitting out oaths and threatening her. Now he was looking warily at her, as though he wasn't sure what to do, or what she was going to do. He only held her gaze for a moment, then he looked away.

'I'll be watching you,' Nell told him quietly. 'Don't start anything again. Don't go off with human girls and make them forget you. That's bad. If I hear you've been doing that I'll get the Watchers on to you. I'll hand you over to them.'

His eyes flickered back to her, and he managed to meet her gaze. 'Really?'

She never even blinked. 'Yes. Really.'

'You might have saved the Elven world,' he said, 'but you haven't freed our families yet.'

'I'm working on it,' she said again. She didn't get the chance to say any more. There was a swish of a long dress and a cold hand touched her shoulder. It was Aurora, standing above her like a living statue. Although even she'd changed. She looked less like marble now.

'What are you doing here?' said Nell.

'Treating Fen.'

'Helping me treat Fen,' interrupted Star, quickly.

'Helping. Yes,' said Aurora with the tiniest of stony smiles. 'His brain is disordered. His thoughts are chaotic. I know the feeling. But he'll become well again eventually.' They both looked down at the handsome but dangerous Elven. 'He'll be a good leader one day. Gwen and I will fix him.' Aurora regarded Gwen. 'Your sister reminds me of myself when I was young – two thousand years ago. I like her.'

Nell swallowed her surprise. But then thought, no, that figures. Gwen is a bit of a goddess, too. 'So you can't stay in the Elven world any more?'

Aurora gave a sigh. 'As it does you, it now poisons us. We stayed away too long. The Vanir are stuck in your world.'

Nell nodded slowly. This was interesting news. This

could make her plan even better. She left Aurora and went back over to Evan.

'I know how to get the camps open. You have to go and get Faolan.'

'Why?'

'You'll see.'

Twenty

A week later Nell stood in the headquarters of the Watchers in London.

This was it. A few minutes from now she'd know if her plan had worked.

Her father had parked his car near the Thames, in a quiet district where the houses on either side were as big as palaces but run down and scruffy now. Dru had led them to a tall, crumbling building at the bottom of a dark street that ended in a set of slippery steps lapped by brown water. The paint on the door was chipped and peeling, so you would think it led into a deserted building. Instead it opened on to a grand hallway with oak panels, gilded mirrors and wide doorways that gave glimpses of bookshelves and buttoned leather chairs. Around them motes of dust danced in the beams of cold wintery sunlight filtering from high windows.

There were five of them. Nell and Evan. Dru and Tom. And Aurora, pale as the snow outside and dressed extravagantly in a huge old-fashioned cloak in dark red velvet. A woman had let them in, told them to wait in the hall and led Dru away.

At first a silence hung over everything, disturbed only by faraway voices murmuring in hushed tones and a door being closed quietly somewhere. Then the argument started. They could see Dru further up the hall, face to face with someone.

'It isn't just me,' the man was shouting. 'Mr Larson will not stand for it.'

Her dad whistled softly, his hands in his pockets. Aurora stared into space, as still as a statue.

As the discussion became louder, Evan picked up an ornate vase from a curly-legged table and examined the bottom. Nell began to scrutinize a dark oil painting on the wall.

'We will not have Elven in our headquarters,' the man said loudly.

Nell felt embarrassed for Evan, but he gave her a sidelong look from under his windswept spiky fringe and winked to show he wasn't bothered.

'And we most definitely will not have a Vanir!' the man continued.

Aurora carried on staring into space. Either she hadn't heard or she was ignoring him.

Other people were listening, though. Heads had started appearing at all the doorways – Watchers who'd been disturbed from their studies and didn't look pleased. Some had keen eyes and looked as though they might carry a gun; others looked like they should be sitting in the leather chairs and reading fairy tales.

'Evan and Aurora are here for discussions only,' she heard Dru saying patiently, as the man paced in front of her. 'You have their word on that.'

The man gave a snort. 'You seem to have forgotten that it's a point of honour amongst Elven to lie to humans!'

That made Evan and Aurora take notice. Aurora's face never altered, but one second she was next to Nell, the next she was in front of the man, her long white hair blowing from the speed of her movement. She tucked a strand behind her ear, as the man cringed back in surprise.

'And you never lie to us?' she said coldly.

The man straightened and brushed a nervous hand down his jacket.

'OK. She can stay.' He swung round and nodded towards Evan. 'But that boy can get out.' He looked at Dru. 'That's an order from a senior Watcher.'

For a few heartbeats Nell thought Dru was going to

tell Evan to go, just to keep the peace, but then she poked the man in the chest.

'No. He's with us. He's part of the deal,' she said loudly, addressing all the Watchers. 'Now, take us to Mr Larson.'

The man's face was a dark corned-beef red now. 'Fine.' He pointed a finger at Evan. 'But anything goes missing and we'll know where to come looking,' he said nastily.

'As if I'd steal anything from here,' Evan said. He waved a hand at the antiques and the old masters scattered around the walls. 'It's nothing compared with what we have.'

He would have said more but Nell dragged him away. 'Don't wind him up any more,' she muttered. 'This is going to get stressful enough as it is.'

They followed her father, Dru and Aurora down the hall to a large room. It had leather chairs and even more gloomy oil paintings on the wall. Most of all, though, it had Stan Larson sitting behind a massive dark wood desk. This was Dru's old boss, the Watcher who would rather lose two human girls than release the Elven from the iron camps. Nell had only met him once before, when she'd rescued Gwen. He didn't care about anything except keeping the Elven away from humans.

He's as bad as the Ice Elven, she thought nervously.

Dru greeted him abruptly, then leaned herself against

the wall, arms folded, ignoring his offer of a seat in one of the leather chairs. Her father began pacing up and down the room. Aurora swept in and sat down in a chair, like a queen on a throne. Nell stood next to Evan, nervously clutching her laptop bag.

Larson watched them suspiciously, leaning forward, his hands steepled together. 'OK. What's going on? If this is a last-ditch attempt to get me to open the camps – forget it. The situation is still too unpredictable.'

'Speak to Nell about that.' Her dad stopped pacing. 'First Dru and I have something to say. We've started our own Watchers' organization. A rival to this one.'

Larson sat back, trying to hide his surprise. 'Ridiculous. The two of you!'

'No, not just us,' said Dru. 'I've contacted my friends, the ones who think like me. Those who didn't like the idea of the camps in the first place. We've had some meetings. There's enough of us who feel the same way.'

'About what?' sneered Larson.

'It was Tom who suggested it,' said Dru. 'The police have to have someone who polices them. To see that they don't become a law unto themselves. We're going to be the Watchers who watch the Watchers.' She walked up to Larson's desk and put her hands down on it and leaned forward. 'We're not supposed to be keeping prisoners.

We're supposed to be keeping the peace – that's all. To see that there's fair play.'

Larson looked like he was sucking a lemon. 'Is that it?'

'No.' Aurora stood up. 'It has to be fair on both sides. I will make sure that the Elven agree to let you visit our world, too. We will allow you through the mists. You'll be fine if you don't stop longer than a night and a day.' She paused. 'But the deal is this – you open the iron camps, now. Today.'

This time Larson smiled. Not because he was pleased, but because he was going to hurt them. 'No. That would take all the governments in the Watcher pact agreeing. And it is too dangerous. We still cannot keep them out of our world. They can still have power over us.'

'They don't want power,' said Dru.

'Leaders would not believe that.' He leaned forward. 'Until we have a way of stopping them coming back into our world, then they have to stay where they are. In the camps.'

He looked round at them all.

'Start your own little Watcher group to watch over us if you have to. It won't make much difference. We won't stop you. But the camps stay.'

Dru looked at Nell. 'Over to you,' she said.

Nell stepped forward nervously and got her laptop

out. Larson watched her as though he was watching a cobra.

'I haven't time for this,' he began.

Nell looked up from the screen. 'Yes, you have,' she said. She swung the laptop round. 'Watch.'

A screen came up. It was video footage from a camcorder. It was inside the Kamchatka camp. A guard could be seen looking from a distance.

'This was taken only this morning.'

Larson had his hands on the desk and he was leaning forward, staring at the screen.

'We'll catch whoever is taking these shots and confiscate the camera.'

'You won't, because it's wolf-powered,' said Nell. 'It's being carried by a wolf called Faolan.' A few grey shapes appeared on either side of the camera, and then there was a lot of howling and baying and snarling as the guard backed off and ran.

'I don't think any of your guards will get near.' Nell looked squarely at Larson. 'We'll record every day. We'll broadcast it on YouTube. Everyone in the world will be able to see it. It'll go viral.'

Larson's lip curled, but Nell could see that a nerve in his eyelid had started twitching. 'No one will believe you. We'll put out that it's a hoax.'

313

'We'll publish the co-ordinates of the camps online.'

Larson's face began to glisten. He was sweating. 'We have ways of stopping people reaching the camps.'

Evan moved and stood next to Nell. 'But you haven't got ways of stopping me.'

Larson looked him up and down. 'And what can you do?' he said. 'You're lucky we're not arresting you on sight.'

Evan didn't even blink. 'Nell said something interesting when she was risking her life to save our world. She said maybe the Elven should stop hiding. We should come out of the mist. Show ourselves to humans. Maybe it is time.'

Larson was shaking with anger now. 'What?' he spat. 'We've kept the secret for hundreds of years and you want to go public.' He gave a harsh laugh.

Evan nodded. 'Yes. Go public. If you don't agree to open the camps immediately, all the Elven who are still free will come out into the open. We'll stop charming humans. We'll let humans remember us. We'll walk through walls in front of everyone.'

'I could arrest you here and now,' growled Larson.

'You're not fast enough,' said Evan. 'But in any case . . .' He turned to Nell. She'd clicked a few buttons whilst he'd been talking and got a Skype connection. Falcon and

Star's faces appeared on the screen.

'Are you two ready?' she said.

Star nodded excitedly. The webcam swung round and showed that they were standing right in the middle of the town centre, near Becca's jewellery shop. 'We're ready to walk straight through this wall, with everyone watching.'

Falcon's face appeared. 'Go on, Evan, let me do it!'

'No!' Larson sprang up. 'Stop!'

'Hang on,' Nell said to them. She clicked back to the video of the iron camp. She hovered her hand over the mousepad. 'Star and Falcon are ready to walk through a wall. And this video is ready to be broadcast everywhere. I just have to click this button. Then the world will see.'

Larson banged his fist on his desk. 'This is blackmail.'

'Yes,' said Evan. He grinned. 'Good plan, isn't it?'

Nell linked her arm through his. 'We thought it up together. Elven and human equals the best.'

Dru leaned forward, her face a few inches from Larson's. 'And we're not leaving until we see the Kamchatka camp opened before our eyes.'

Larson looked like he wanted to be sick. 'Wait,' he said. 'Don't do anything. I have to go and talk to someone.'

He marched out of the room.

For a moment, they were all silent, and then very quietly, like children in a classroom misbehaving before the teacher came back, they began dancing round the office, sniggering and hugging each other. Even Aurora joined in.

It took a few more hours. They refused to leave. They sat in Larson's office. Watchers came and looked in now and then. Some scowled. Some gave them the thumbs-up. Larson hurried by a few times, looking harassed. They heard shouting coming from a meeting room.

Then finally someone came and called them through to a large room with a big white screen at the front. It was displaying a webcam link-up to the iron camp. Nell heard Evan catch his breath. She reached for his hand. He was shaking.

Larson strode forward. 'You win, Dru,' he said sourly. 'Kamchatka is to be opened. It will be a trial. See how it goes.'

'I didn't win,' said Dru. She glanced at Nell proudly. 'It was all my granddaughter's idea.'

Nell grinned back. Then her dad squeezed her shoulder. 'I hope this teaches you a lesson,' he said to Larson. 'Never argue with Nell.'

Her dad was proud of her! Whatever next?

'Never mind that,' she said. 'Get the camp open, before I die of excitement.'

Larson spoke. 'OK. Stand the guards down. Open the

gates. Arrange transport.' Then he stood back, with his arms folded.

The camera swung round and she could see all the Elven standing in a group. They must have been listening to Larson's instructions over a loudspeaker. There was a delay of a few seconds and then they all started cheering and hugging each other.

She could feel Evan fidgeting beside her.

'Request that Duck Rivers is held up to the camera,' he said to Larson. 'I have a message for her.'

Larson sighed and did as he was told. They heard the message distantly relayed to the waiting Elven. Nothing happened for a minute, and then suddenly a laughing Elven face shot up into view, as though boosted from below. It was a little girl, maybe five years old, with a whoosh of white hair sticking up as though she'd touched a static ball.

'Duck!' Evan shot forward and touched the screen. 'Yea! Duck!'

His little sister. The one he hadn't seen for years. And behind, the out-of-focus faces of his parents.

'Happy birthday, Duck!'

Nell heaved a sigh of relief. They'd done it.

317

Twenty-one

It was Sunday. They'd just finished lunch. Upstairs, in her bedroom, Nell had everything ready for the new school term tomorrow. The snow was still deep outside, but the bitter cold had faded. Normal life was about to resume.

But not just yet.

Real life could still be on hold for a while longer.

She looked around the table. It was not only her and Gwen and Mum for dinner, like usual. Evan was there, too. She grinned. He was squirming a little and embarrassed, but her mum had insisted.

Nell had introduced them yesterday. No bees had buzzed, Evan had let Jackie remember him. After he'd gone, Jackie said thoughtfully, 'He might be a bit too wild for you. He's like some of the gypsy boys we deal with, intriguing and fascinating but much too tricky.' She had stopped, puzzled. 'Although I can see he's very sweet, in a slightly worrying way.'

'Forget everything but that he's sweet,' Nell had told her.

One day the Elven would come out of the mists. She'd make it happen. One day her mum would know the truth about Evan, but not now.

A week had passed since the visit to London. The camps were being opened. The Elven, a little weak and sick after so much exposure to iron, were going home. The conflict between the Elven and the Watchers had been called off.

Eight more Watchers had come and joined Dru and Tom in his house. That's where their new headquarters were. No more Red House with its iron protection. This was a place where the Elven could come and meet as well. It was being made official. They would police the Watchers from now on.

She smiled happily to herself. And she would continue to live between the two worlds.

'OK. Who's clearing up?' said Jackie.

'Oops. Got unfinished homework from last term,' said Gwen and disappeared.

Nell grabbed Evan's hand. 'Time for us to disappear too.' Through the mist, she added silently.

Bees buzzed and in an instant her mum forgot about *both* of them, and started stacking the dishwasher herself.

An hour later they were hand in hand, making their way through the snowy wonderland of the Elven forest, towards the palace.

Nell couldn't stop laughing that she'd managed to trick her mum.

'Not fair,' said Evan. 'You're learning all our tricks.'

When they got close enough to see the palace nestled in amongst the trees, Nell stopped, suddenly unsure of herself.

'Is everyone settling in OK?' she asked.

The Elven had been in the camps a long time. Maybe it would be strange to be free again. Maybe they would hate her for being human.

Evan grinned. 'They're fine. We're not. It's back to us having to do what the adults say. So lots of arguments. They say we've gone feral. But they're still pretty weak, so when they yell we just run off and do what we want, as usual.'

Nell hesitated. 'You sure your mama doesn't mind me visiting? It must be pretty new to them.'

'They're getting used to the idea,' he said, diplomatically. 'Slowly.'

'What do they think about coming through the mist to our world and not hiding any more?'

'My dad says it's about time. But it scares them. It'll take time.'

'Yea, Evan!' shouted a little voice.

It was Duck. She'd been sitting on the doorstep waiting for them, and she came running through the trees. Nell was introduced and fell straight under the little Elven girl's spell.

They walked along, swinging her by her hands between them as she went *wheeeee*. Just before the clearing they passed a little pool at the side of the path. Nell stopped. It had frozen over but the water was so crystal-clear that the ice was like a mirror, and reflected their faces perfectly.

Her hair was still fair. Evan's had gone a shade darker. And his eyes had lightened from charcoal to dark silver.

'Look at us. We're unique,' she said. 'Half Elven, half human, half ice.' She smiled at his reflected face. 'If anyone's going to let the human world know that the Elven are real, it's us.'

He spun her round so that they were face to face. 'You really think it could happen? We could live openly?'

She put her arms round him. 'Yes. It'll have to come true – if we're going to go out with each other, properly.'

Evan grinned. Then he looked down at Duck. 'Go and find Star and tell her we're here. I've got something to talk to Nell about, on our own.' The little girl ran off happily.

Nell wondered for a moment what he was going to say. But he didn't say anything.

He kissed her for the second time.

Find out how Nell and Evan's story began in

MIST

Read on for an exclusive extract . . .

One

Don't go into the wood after dark. Her mother's warning echoed in her head, but Nell ignored it.

Shadows flickered in the corner of her eye and the trees creaked and groaned in the cold wind, making the hairs on the back of her neck stand up in alarm. The wood was ancient. It spread out for miles behind her house, dark and secretive. If she stared into it, it seemed to stare back. If she ran down the narrow paths, branches grabbed at her like twiggy hands.

She was heading for the darkest part of all, where the ground dropped into a hollow and the path became stepping stones over marshy ground. It used to have an iron fence all the way round, but recently someone had torn it down.

Mist filled the hollow like smoke in a dish and never went away. The dampness caused the trees all around to be covered with ivy and mosses that hung like hair from the branches. As she walked down the slope into the mist, she began to think she could hear a ghostly music, right on the edge of her hearing, as though someone was playing something old-fashioned, like a harp.

That wasn't all she could hear. Somewhere in the woods something was howling. A thousand years ago it would've been a wolf, now it was probably a Staffie belonging to one of the boys who liked to think they were gangsters. They brought the dogs into the woods to train, making them dangle off branches by their teeth, and then wielding them at people like weapons. Hopefully the warden who patrolled the woods would go after them and not notice her.

She was following someone else. Her mystery boy.

He was somewhere ahead of her, very close. He was the reason she was creeping through the trees, instead of at home, out of school uniform, enjoying tea and a little Princess Zelda.

She jumped on to the first stepping stone, the mist swirling around her and settling on her face like tiny pearls. Then on to the next. There were twenty stones across the bottom of the hollow, the ground either side soggy and covered in brambles. She had a brief vision of falling and breaking her ankle. Would anyone think to look for her down here? No, because hardly anyone came this far. She would die a lonely, painful death, and Gwen, her sister, would hang a school scarf and a bunch of flowers from a nearby tree, a sad reminder of a young life lost. Although if it happened to Gwen then there'd be a whole bank of flowers and little messages from her sobbing friends saying Rest in Peace Angel, we all miss you.

She reached the last stone and stopped. Mystery boy had disappeared. That was impossible – she'd seen him walk into the mist, skipping oddly from stepping stone to stepping stone as though he'd decided to play a complicated game of hopscotch. So where was he? Unless he was brambleproof or he'd sunk in the mud, he should be ahead of her.

A twig snapped like a gunshot.

'Nell Church?'

She froze. He was behind her and that wasn't in the plan. He wasn't supposed to actually see or speak to her. She prayed for invisibility or the end of the world, whichever was quicker, but it didn't happen. So she turned around and he was there, vivid in the twilit mist. How many fourteen-year-old boys had skin as pale as milk as though they'd never seen the sun, hair so white it looked bleached and eyes as black as charcoal? Add to that the small silver earring glittering in one ear, and the small tattoo of a wolf's head on the inside of one of his skinny white wrists. Who *was* he?

'If you wanted to ask me out, you could've done it at school,' he said, with his crooked grin, the one that drove her crazy. His accent wasn't local, it was singsong and breathy, maybe a little bit Irish or Scottish, but not really like either. He just sounded like no one else she knew.

He'd started at Woodbridge Community College last week, and it seemed that no one except her noticed that he hardly attended any lessons. Instead he spent his time watching the Woodbridge students as though he was a prince and school was a strange ritual he'd never come across before. And the more no one noticed him, the more he started showing off, rolling out of cupboards during maths lessons or walking across the stage during assembly. His face and name slipped out of everyone's mind, except hers. All she knew was that each morning he came out of the woods and each afternoon he went back in there. Her house backed on to the woods, and she'd watched him from her bedroom window, wandering out in the mornings, yawning and leaning over the fence to pinch an apple from the neighbour's tree. Then in the afternoon he'd go running and leaping back down the bramble-covered paths as though he couldn't wait for the woods to swallow him again.

'Sorry, I wasn't, I didn't . . .' she began.

'Joking,' he said.

She felt a blush start to storm up her face. 'Oh. Of course.'

A silence fell. Top of the class, yet she couldn't think of one single thing to say to start a conversation. Unlike Gwen, who failed all exams but who'd happily chat away to an alien if one landed and was cute enough.

'Don't you know it's dangerous near the mist?' he said. 'People disappear and are never seen again.'

He was teasing her. Maybe she deserved it for following him so clumsily.

'And don't you know the woods are private?' she said, grasping at straws. 'You'll get done for trespassing.' Stupid, ridiculous thing to say. Did he look like the sort of boy who would care? No.

He jumped a stepping stone closer, gazing at her through his spiky fringe, head angled to one side. 'Woods don't belong to anyone, except Gaia.'

'If that's another name for Woodbridge Council, then yes,' she said.

He laughed, which was something. Usually no one got her jokes. Now he was watching her curiously.

'So why did you follow me?' he said.

She quickly tried to think of a plausible excuse for being here in the wood, with its reputation for being dangerous at night. Not one single idea came to her rescue, so she had to confess the truth.

'If I see something that puzzles me I have to find out about it.'

It was true – not knowing about anything drove her crazy. Maybe she'd inherited a detective gene from her police officer mum, but Gwen claimed it was because she was obsessive. Even as a little girl, if she half saw a street sign or a notice or a poster in the street, she'd *have* to go back and read it all.

'I'm especially attracted to weird or creepy things,' she finished.

The twisty grin appeared again. 'Which am I?'

She concentrated on kicking at one of the white stones. 'Erm. Weird.' She glanced up. He didn't seem bothered she'd just called him a freak. So she carried on. 'I had to find out – who are you?'

He thought about that. 'I'm a boy who doesn't exist,' he said, eventually.